To Tony [handwritten inscription]

"m" [handwritten]

Lee Shearer [signature]

HIDING IN DES MOINES

****

BY

LEE SHEARER

First published by Createspace, Inc. on

ISBN: 0615658334
ISBN 13: 9780615658339

Library of Congress Control Number: 2012910990
Printed in the United States of America

ACKNOWLEDGMENTS

*****

Creative fiction writing is challenging, frustrating, and hard work. It's ups and downs are hard to explain till you have experienced them. Frustrations and self doubts are a constant companion. The self satisfaction of completing a fictional journey and receiving some kind words for the efforts are rewarding and exhilarating. On this kind of journey, a writer needs good friends and companions.

Thanks to my wife Dianna who always is supportive and a friend. She finds a way to stimulate my imagination, loves my humor (even when it's lame), and encourages me when I want to quit. Life is good with a soulmate by your side.

My friend Dennis Young, a retired Executive Vice President and CFO of Well Fargo Financial, made the process fun. His advice on humor, story twists and portraying an accurate positive image of Des Moines was invaluable. Good friends are hard to find and are treasured.

Bill Sheridan, of Sheridan Writes, LLC, was invaluable on editing challenges and provided fun encouragement from a fellow writer. Hope we got them all!!

To my 94 year old Mother, Harryet, thanks for giving me the love of reading. To my 95 year old Father, Jess, thanks for the inspiration that anything is possible with hard work and blind faith.

AUTHOR BIOGRAPHY

*****

Leon (Lee) Shearer has been an attorney in the Des Moines area for over 40 years. He was the co-founder of Shearer, Templer and Pingel. He entered semi-retirement from his role as Vice-President and General Counsel of Pioneer Hi-Bred International, Inc when that NYSE company merged with DuPont. He has failed retirement.

He has co-authored two construction law books and many nationally published articles on technical legal subjects.

Hiding In Des Moines involves a retiring vigilante for hire who has used Des Moines as his hiding place for over a decade. He struggles with retirement and the absence of the rush of his long term occupation. One last job, his biggest and most complex, presents an irresistible opportunity. It involves stopping a merger between a Mexican drug cartel and a huge Iowa based pot operation. Eliminating the leaders earns a bonus.

Underlying this fast pace story is a secondary theme of the emotions, challenges and frustrations of retirement and aging and the need for constantly developing new chapters of life.

Shearers first mystery novel *Cycles of Death* involved a group of aging business men who go on RAGBRAI, a nationally known bike ride across Iowa. In the process they discover a serial killer has been using the ride as a hunting ground for female victims. The amateur detectives break numerous laws but discover the culprits. Since the legal system is not available as the evidence is flawed they must deal with the matter.

It's available at L.R. Shea Publishing, Inc 31634 Silverado, Waukee, Iowa 50263 for $14.00 plus $2.00 shipping.

Shearer has become a relentless researcher on the subject of aging. In the fall of 2012 look for a new interactive web site, *Energized Aging. com.* It will feature observations and suggestions on energized aging with articles from experts in anti-aging medicine, plastic surgery, primary care medicine, finance, and mental health. Also included will be articles on developing challenging hobbies, new careers, successful weight loss and physical conditioning. These are all directed to the reader who wants aging to be a chronological occurrence not a psychologically controlling event.

Follow this process on *Lee-Shearer.com*

Retirement-What Is It? Will I Know It If I See It? Can I Do It?

****

PART ONE

"First You Forget Their Names, Then You Forget Their Faces, Then You Forget To Zip Up, And Then You Forget To Unzip."

BRANCH RICKEY

PRELUDE

"Should I Go On Playing Bridge And Dining, Going In The Same Old Monotonous Circles? It's Easy That Way, But It's A Sort Of Suicide Too."

ANTOINETTE PERRY

*****

THE TIRES OF THE ANTIQUE red 320i BMW convertible crunched on the frost accumulating on the road. The sharp crackling echoed through the night like a string of exploding lady-finger firecrackers. The car fishtailed as the driver braked and pulled into the Woodward, Iowa train station, which had long ago been abandoned by the Northwestern Railway. It was now used as a picnic center at the western end of the Woodward High Trestle Bike Trail. Purple and white pipe lights illuminated the sign describing the 25 mile ride from Woodward to Ankeny, Iowa. The colors were coordinated with the lighting of the varied angled steel art work surrounding the thirteen floor high half-mile long trestle bridge running over the Des Moines River Valley. The art work was designed to create an impression of entering a coal mine, which were prevalent in the area.

The night was cold and the wind still, with frost settling on the trees. The moon and stars illuminated the scene like early dawn not deep night. Deer stopped to watch. Their nocturnal grazing was interrupted.

A small man got out of his convertible. With a great deal of effort, he removed a bicycle from the back seat. The leather seat ripped. He didn't notice or even care. He tugged and removed the black Trek 790 from its unusual angle in the back seat. He paused to put on his helmet and riding gloves, and pushed off. His movements were quick and effortless. He started down the trail with the ease of an experienced rider. Avoiding ice patches was no problem. The crackling from the breaking frost increased with every rotation of the tires. It echoed through the silent night. Deer jumped in varied directions and ran for cover.

The 2.6 miles to the Trestle were quickly traversed. The hard pumping rider sped by the tall monument commemorating the early immigrant coal miners of the area. Midway across the half mile long bridge, the freezing temperature of the ride and the purple and white lights outlining the steel frames of the High Trestle Bridge sent a start through the lone rider. He skidded to a stop.

What am I doing here? I am freezing! Where am I? Suddenly his mind was fully functioning. He recognized the Des Moines River Valley some 150 feet below. The light of the moon made it appear as a long wandering silver ribbon. The trees and rocks strewn in varied clusters across the half-mile wide bottom of the valley sparkled from the frost and the moon light.

A serene smile came across his face. He stopped shivering. He reached into his bike pouch and removed the cork from the bottle of Templeton Rye. He downed two quick full swallows. Slowly he mounted the four foot high steel guard rail. He stood balanced for a full two minutes. He drew in several deep breathes of the crisp air. Two more deep pulls of Rye followed. His head slowly rotated and absorbed the sights of the moon illuminated valley meandering to the south as far as he could see. He raised his head and looked at the full moon for 30 seconds, a smile frozen on his face. He then performed a perfect swan dive off the rail, disappearing into the night. Never once did he utter a sound or make a move to avoid the rocks rushing up at him.

The screech of the wind by his ears, the increasing sensation of speed, and the surreal sight of the rocks rushing at him was dreamlike. For a brief second he felt so very alive. He did not release the smile. He never flinched. His decision had been made. He had to do this while he still had matters in his own control.

THE SCORE FOR TIM O'BRIEN WAS A PERFECT 10 FOR FORM AND STYLE, BUT ZERO FOR THE LANDING.

CHAPTER ONE

"If You Want To Feel Young, Agile And Smart, Take An Ocean Cruise For Retirees."

LEE SHEARER

*****

THE HALF MOON'S florescent beams were dancing like ghost across the waves of the unusually calm North Atlantic. Jane Marie Beam of Forest City, Iowa slowly sipped on her first glass of LeCrema Chardonnay. Her mind was giddy. She felt ashamed of how she felt standing nude on the balcony of her state room. The anticipation of another erotic night moving to the rhythm of the waves with her new friend, Neil Barrett III, sent shivers pulsing throughout her 55 year old body. Feelings long forgotten now were returning with vivid intensity. Like riding a bike, some things come back quickly.

She filled her lungs with another deep-salty scented breath and moved from the balcony into her large highest deck room. It was time to dress for dinner. She was now free from the constraints of being the wife of a wealthy, stuffy, small town businessman. No more prying eyes of nosy neighbors. No more company parties and the required sucking up to the opinionated owner, Homer Harger, and his boring ever so proper wife. No more laughing at stale jokes and agreeing with

1

self-important stories. Too bad Albert had not lived long enough to enjoy this freedom.

Giggling like a teenager, she felt a long way from the 4300 people of Forest City, Iowa. Its heavily wooded rolling hills and stately homes were a far cry from the opulent surrounding on the cruise. The small college atmosphere provided by Waldorf College and well educated friends had made it a delightful home for raising the three girls, but for a single woman it had many drawbacks. Her conduct the last three days, especially the nights, would have put the town in an uproar as lewd gossip would spread like a prairie fire. She felt a pang of guilt. Maybe it was lust?

She was like a prisoner being released to enjoy a new world. Three years as a caregiver to Albert had frozen her feelings. She had no sexual desires during that entire time as the days blended into years. She should not feel guilty, but she often did. She was enjoying recapturing the thrill of being courted, the fun of flirting, the warmth of growing close and maybe even the lust.

The cruise along the east coast of Canada on the very expensive Opulent Voyager was proving to be all she had imagined. Even though she was alone, she had enjoyed every minute of the first two stops at Montreal and Quebec City. The subtle feelings of lonesomeness were appearing less frequently. She slowly stopped thinking like a fifth wheel or an odd number.

In Montreal Tim and Jackie, from upper Michigan, had coupled up with her. They were her age and obviously alive, curious, and in love. The two walked with her through Old Montreal. They wandered though the Place d'Armes to the Royal Bank. The elegance of the Cours Le Royer and St. Jacques were breathtaking. They exchanged pleasantries about their children and grandchildren. It all came to an awkward silence when the death of her husband came up. The silence was deafening. People are uneasy discussing death and the lingering emotions of the living.

In Quebec City she walked the streets of Place Royal with a new couple, Bart and Tanya, from Minneapolis. Tanya was a wealth of knowledge. Bart was filled with constant political jokes. He had vivid distain for any Democrat office holder or candidate. Together they explored the site of the New France settlement by horse-drawn carriage.

The walk over the Plains of Abraham Battlefield Park was moving. As she looked down the tree filled cliffs to the beach below, Jane could literally envision the French, Indians, and English fighting for control of this early toe-hold in America.

Jane took another intoxicating deep breath before shutting the door to her stateroom. The widow was learning to move on. She still had her sad moments even though a year had passed since Albert's death and his three years of slow degeneration. As she watched the many infirmed cruise guests trying to live for one more fun experience, her mind would always drift back to him.

Albert's engineering skills had led him to significant wealth as a key engineer in designing multiple new variations for upgrading and personalizing RV's. The Winnebago founder, John Hanson, had recognized his flair for the unusual, but could never entice him to leave HHH Industries. Harry "Homerun" Harger had mentored him through college and had an almost hypnotic control over his thoughts and actions. After 30 years of keeping up with the constant changes of models and the unrelenting pressure from Homerun, Albert became terminally ill from incessant cigarette smoking, incredibly long hours, pressure for immediate production, and a poor immune system.

The rollercoaster of varied and conflicting feelings from her past few years were still with her every day. She was trying to find a path forward to enjoying life and feeling positive again. Neil was like a Five Hour Energy Drink for her emotional state and self image.

The way they met was serendipitous. The tall, slender, younger stranger had grabbed the last seat beside her on the jet boat ride through the Reversing Rapids at St. Johns, Nova Scotia. The Reversing Rapids were a unique phenomena. The Atlantic tide roared into the Bay of Fundy at such a rapid pace that the flow of water from the St. John River to the sea actually reversed itself. A 15 foot water fall flowing east to the sea actually was engulfed and became 20 feet below the surface as it met the incoming tides. The swirling waters, where the falls came crashing into the incoming tide, created a frightening sight: whirling pools, huge frothing waves, and smashing multi-directional currents.

The frightening site was a key cruise attraction for that stop. Long yellow jet boats driven by Canadian kamikaze pilots drove full speed into the swirling pools with their 500 horse power motors roaring. Waves gushed over the passengers heads as the boat shot under the wave, and then surfaced speeding atop the next series of waves. They looked like a large trout hooked on feathered fly breaking water.

"Neil Barrett from Minneapolis," he remarked as the ride ended. His broad smile, sharp-featured face, deep tan, and beautiful black hair were immediately captivating.

He gently held her arm and helped her totally soaked body out of the yellow jet boat and on to the dock.

"That was quite a thrill. When we went into that twenty foot whirl-pool, you almost broke my hand. How about a hot coffee half filled with a little Yukon Jack to warm us up?"

Jane had not even remembered reaching for and squeezing his hand as the boat shot full speed into the swirling pools and under the huge waves. She only remembered the sudden rush of fear and then exhilaration from conquering that fear. After the hour long ride, all the drenched passengers went to the rustic changing rooms, quickly put on dry clothing, and bagged their salt water soaked clothes. The chill of the September breeze against cold soaked flesh made her shiver. Goose bumps appeared on every inch of her body.

After a coffee, well laced with a sweet orange tasting Yukon Jack whiskey, the two new friends felt their insides glowing despite the cool temperature. Neil moved closer to her as they sat down in the ancient white tour bus.

"We would be warmer if we rode back with my arm around you. I don't want to appear fresh, but I'm cold too. What's your name, and where are you from young lady?"

She knew the young lady line was pure male BS and a lame line. She nodded and slid close. Jane was shocked at how easy it was to talk to him. He asked all the right questions and responded to all of her remarks with interest and humor. She felt like a teenager, knowing full well he was trying to seduce her. She was light hearted and anxious to spend more time with him. He was a far cry from the unmarried men of Forest City, Iowa.

The afternoon blended into the evening. They both were a little under the influence of Yukon Jack, and made a date for the eight o'clock dinner seating. When she got back to her stateroom she felt like a fool. A happy excited fool, realizing she had spilled her guts to a total stranger.

Jane was stunned by her behavior as she dressed for their first date. She put on a black laced bra and matching thong. She selected a black dress with a plunging neckline and split skirt. She had never worn them before. They had been bought at a frivolous moment just before the trip. She was hoping she would find a chance to wear them and pull her out of the doldrums of her life. They worked.

She arrived at the table. It was set for two, not the usual eight, and was located in a dim corner with a view of the rolling sea. A bottle of her favorite chardonnay was cooling. Neil arrived in a dark suit, expensive white shirt, and red and gold tie. His shining black hair hung to his collar top. The dark complexion, deep brown eyes, and late evening beard looked right out of a GQ magazine. He was more handsome than she remembered. The smell and touch made her skin quiver.

The evening drifted into the night. Her inhibitions disappeared at the same pace as the wine was consumed. At the end of the meal, she could hardly wait to get him back to her stateroom. The evening that followed was mesmerizing. She felt like she was literally floating on the ceiling watching her own body tangled with Neil's well muscled six-foot frame. She could not believe what she was seeing and feeling. His soft touch gliding endlessly over her caused long dominant endorphins to be released at an overwhelming pace.

Her years of abstinence caused a flood of animal energy and a pent up need erupting from deep within her. Neil kept up with her newly released needs as only a man 20 years younger than her could do.

The next two days were the same. Each morning she swore not to be a fool and not to try to screw him every time they met. Each day she failed like an alcoholic working in a liquor store. Her libido was roaring, and his intensity was amazing.

Jane took a deep breath and looked into the mirror. She had to get ready. They had scheduled to meet for a drink on the fantail before dinner at their private place. The red dress she had just bought in the ships over-priced boutique clung tight to her very trim body. The countless hours of exercise and body-building had caused her five-six body to become curved and powerful. The breasts augmentation work had tilted the twins towards the sky, not the ground. The brow-lift and wrinkle removal from around her mouth and eyes by a very expensive plastic surgeon had done their job. She was slim, trim, and ready for action.

She sprayed her shoulder length dark brown hair into perfect form and fluffed her breasts up so they provided ample cleavage above her dress top. Then she noticed the note that had been slid under her door.

She opened it with a smile, expecting another surprise from Neil. Her eyes froze and the tears welled into Bambi-like tears. He had left the boat and was returning to his wife, whom he had failed to mention. She fell into the chair, reached for a drink, and cried without remorse. Little did she know her life had just been saved!

THE BLAZING ORANGE SUN WAS SINKING INTO THE SEA. The breeze was sharp and cool for a late September evening. Jim Moore of Sauk Center, Minnesota, aka Neil Barrett, Rich Carson, John Timmons and Richard Wheat, was quietly having a double vodka gimlet on the rocks in the shadows of the ship's fantail bar. He leaned against the rail, flicked his cigar ashes and repeatedly looked at his watch. Where was that stupid old broad? He was going to miss the company of this one. She actually was smart and funny when not consumed with her survivor's guilt. She also had been a great lay. He had never before experienced the floating butterfly position.

He was frustrated. He had told her twice to meet him for a drink in their special place to watch the sun set from the shadows by the bar. He heard a noise behind him. Without concern, he noticed the small dark skinned waiter approach him with another gimlet. The waiter's large black eyes were piercing and focused. His movement was swift and cat-like. His head was constantly shifting to assure they were alone.

Suddenly, Moore felt his six-foot frame floating in air hurdling towards the 30 degree black water below. His scream was muffled by the band's music. In a few seconds he disappeared in the wake of the ship's powerful twin propellers leaving him behind for a slow but certain death.

He had approximately 20 minutes to live. His body quivered with fear as he struggled to stay afloat, energy ebbing out of his rapidly cooling muscles. He kept screaming, and thinking that he had to live. This had been his biggest score to date. He had every one of her stock account numbers and passwords. When he got to the ship's computer bank after dinner and two hours of sex with the 55 year old cougar, the accounts would be drained into his off shore Bermuda accounts in 30

6

seconds. She was supposed to be in the water dying an inch at a time like the others. Not him.

The lights of the speeding ship were fading dots on the horizon. The moon provided little light as Moore struggled with whining gasps to avoid sliding into the depth of the Atlantic. His muscles were becoming tight, the sea water filled his throat and his breaths were short and rapid. He panicked as he knew he was dying.

Doug Valli stood quietly on the fantail of the ship and downed the undelivered gimlet in one swallow, while watching his stolen waiter's jacket floating into the sea. He smiled and gave a salute to the watery grave of Jim Moore. Valli's kiss-off note had crushed the ego of the gorgeous lady in suite 1099. She would never know it was the reason she was alive and might love another day.

Valli leaned against the rail and looked at the disappearing bobbing black dot. He reflected on the events that had happened in less than three seconds. He felt no remorse for ending a life. He knew the Mason, Terry, Hart and Clark families wished Moore would swim forever in hell. He had forever taken someone from each of them. Debra Mason never returned to her ship from a tourist shopping trip to St. Thomas. Nina Terry mysteriously was found wedged in a deep crevasse of a glacier after a helicopter ride to the top as part of a ship excursion at Juneau. Monica Hart simply never disembarked from her ship on the cruise from New York to London. Martha Clark was deemed a suicide based on her note. Her body was never found after the cruise from Honolulu to Tahiti.

"By the way Jim, bad things happen to bad people. The four cruise lines that helped me locate you have paid a nice fee for assurance that you are enjoying learning how to become a marathon swimmer."

Calmly he walked to his room and slipped into a black pin striped suit. As he wandered to the piano bar, his mind wandered to his first and only love. He wondered how young Mindy Browski would like a cruise with 400 old people like him. He enjoyed a glass of Panther Creek syrah before ordering a fresh lobster the size of a purse dog and a warm spinach salad loaded with anchovies.

This kind of day always gave him an appetite. The adrenaline was still working. This time it was so easy. He chuckled. Jim Boy was so smug and so surprised at being caught. This was kill number 49. He couldn't help but wonder if this would be last such celebration?

CHAPTER TWO

"Expecting The World To Treat You Fairly Because You Are A Good Person Is A Little Like Expecting A Bull Not To Attack Because You Are A Vegetarian."

DENNIS WHOLEY

✶✶✶✶✶

JANE BEAM'S TRIP to Forest City was slow and full of mood swings. Her memories of the cruise, the crazy experience with Neil, and the emotions of being unceremoniously dumped by a short note slid under her door kept her mind spinning. After hours of travel, she had come to grips with her emotions. She knew she had crawled out of her widowhood shell. She had experienced and closed another chapter of life. She felt very alive. She was still young, vital and healthy. She recognized her need to find a new life. She craved new experiences, challenges and emotions. She put the self pity mood away and finished her second glass of wine.

The safe boring world of being a rich widow in Forest City, Iowa was about to be viewed in the rear view mirror. No more dates with older widowers, multiple divorced abusers or perpetually single nerds. She had to move on and away.

Little did she know she was lucky to be alive rather than shark food in the Atlantic. Jane had been given another chance to live and experience the multiple opportunities of life thanks to Valli fulfilling his last contract.

THE TRIP BACK TO DES MOINES after a quick productive stay on the cruise ship was tiring. After the ship docked at Newport, Rhode Island, Valli wandered around the rich surroundings. He bought a handmade shawl and very expensive pearl necklace as a wedding gift for his young love. After a dozen fresh oysters and a pan fried cod dinner, he rented a car and drove to New York. He was unusually relaxed. The drive was slow and beautiful. As he expertly navigated the tight curving road, he marveled at the massive ancient trees which were filled with mixed colors of red, orange, and yellow. He repeatedly found himself taking deep breathes of the cool clean air. It was good to be alive.

The ship's computer entry system, designed to keep track of its passengers, would never miss him as he had never registered. He had boarded on a security pass provided by the cruise line and used a room which the computer showed as unoccupied.

He gave very little thought to having saved the attractive widow from Iowa or the elimination of the gigolo turned murderer. It was his last project. He felt at ease and content with having again delivered justice to an aggrieved family; in this case four families. Their retainer was now deemed earned.

Brief stops in New York, Miami, and Memphis using different names and passports were necessary to avoid any tracing of his movement. He was known as Arturo Ricci in his birth place of Palermo. By being meticulous and overly cautious, he had survived to the ripe age of 69 and prospered in a dangerous vocation.

His business of selling justice was a family tradition. The Ricci family had a long history in the rise, fall, and eventual resurrection of the Mafia in Sicily. This family had survived various changes of dominance and control in Palermo for centuries. Their ancestors had watched as their island changed hands like a Monopoly game card. The Phoenicians had used its many deep accessible harbors as haven for numerous fleets. The Carthaginians sent Hannibal to conquer it after Himera had failed to suppress the fierce fighters of this sparse Island.

The Romans and Byzantine empires later dominated the island and pillaged the populace. The Vandals, Moors, and Normans all had used and abused this resilient island's residents. The Ricci lineage had always been on the side of the abused yet resolved survivors.

The Ricci family's modern history began with the dominance of Sicily by Spain during the sixteenth century. Spanish control was briefly interrupted by Napoleon's conquest of Naples; Sicily was thrown in like a Monopoly card as part of the peace treaty. With Napoleon's subsequent defeat at Waterloo, King Ferdinand again claimed Sicily for Spain. The Ricci family, known for their enterprising efforts and resilience, was a significant part of the Spanish development of the island's businesses infrastructure. They quickly built their wealth, power and political influence.

The last power switch impacting this ravaged Island occurred in 1860 when Giuseppe Garibaldi united the various Italian City States and multiple countries on the Italian peninsula to form the Republic of Italy. Sicily was one of the last areas to fall. The famed Mille Army of Garibaldi combined with the rebellious local Sicilian farmers and seized control of Palermo and eventually the entire island. Garibaldi rewarded his ally rebels by systematically either killing or imprisoning them. As taxes and abuses again were imposed, the modern Mafia evolved with the Ricci family as a key element.

This loose organization of families had been in existence for centuries. Its purpose was to serve as the Robin Hood to the poor people of Sicily. Their vicious swift attacks on individuals to protest government abuse or wrongs committed by the wealthy created an atmosphere of fear that actually moderated intolerable action against the poor. The populace protected the families from discovery and paid tributes for their protection. Governments ignored their crimes in fear of vengeance and for appropriate pay-offs.

The Ricci family saw the profit from the business of selling protection, and their personal wealth grow dramatically during the post-Garibaldi era. Arturo's grandfather's, Miliano, portion of the approved operations was in Palermo. His primary business was collecting the protection fees for the growing business and commercial companies in the wealthy area of Viale Della Liberta and all other areas running east to the ocean. As a sideline, the Ricci family also ran all prostitution in the area. In addition, they controlled the docks and all smuggling of stolen goods into and out of Palermo. The Ricci men were notorious for being hands-on managers when it came to the prostitution enterprise, especially when evaluating new talent.

The family's wealth and power grew significantly until the 1930's and the arrival of Mussolini. The Ducci's fascist regime feared and hated the families of the Mafia organization. This loose knit group of independent dispensers of protection was a serious barrier to Mussolini's control of the populace of this continuously rebellious island. Even though Mussolini sought to find and eliminate them by violent family attacks, bribes, and coercion, he never dominated them. Three of Arturos's uncles died in this purge.

Arturo's father, Antonio, survived the soldiers of Mussolini and, in fact, helped turn the situation into an opportunity. He and other surviving family members negotiated an arrangement with the Allied forces during WWII. This arrangement was negotiated through the infamous Lucky Luciano, who had prospered as a Mafia leader in New York after leaving Palermo.

It was not an accident that the Allied forces conquered Sicily in thirty-nine days. The locations of the enemy's power, transportation, and reserves were pinpointed by the family's scouts and spies. In each town a prearranged representative met the Allied forces and provided them with perfect information.

Palermo was a disaster from the bombings and fighting. The Allies, true to their promises, directed a steady flow of cash for rebuilding and left behind abundant amounts of supplies and equipment. Virtually all of these resources fell into the hands of their Mafia allies. Because of this new found, nearly unlimited, treasure trove of material and funding for rebuilding, the families quickly rebounded and created the new business: the black-market sale of war surplus items. Little of the rebuilding funds went to the designated projects. After the war, the payback continued when the Allies selected the Administrator of Sicily, Don Calegero Vizzini. He was the designee of the Mafia. For years the wealth of the Ricci family grew to untold levels.

Arturo was born in 1943, during the bombing of Palermo. Patton's and Montgomery were racing up the east and west coasts of Sicily. He recalled little of those dangerous times, but his family's distrust for anyone in power permeated his development. He learned the family business during his teenage years by collecting protection fees from the elite shops on Viela Della Liberta. As they handed over the fee, the owners always offered a feeble smile as they paid for their protection. Arturo felt sorry for them as there was no need for protection; the families controlled all crime and the police.

In his late teenage years, he and his father regularly quarreled about the injustice of taking from the poor for protection that was not needed. Antonio dismissed all challenges from his belligerent son. It was their right to take such funds for their past and future protection. After one of the more aggressive disputes, Arturo announced he was through with the business of bleeding the poor and left Palermo for the wonders of Rome.

His playboy life in Rome was one of non-stop womanizing and drinking, all in keeping with the Ricci tradition. Unfortunately, it ended with conscription into the Italian Army when he was involved in a drunken brawl that sent three policemen to the hospital. At first he hated the army's authority and regimentation. He found an escape by volunteering for the Elite Black Band training. In the process of becoming a member of this unit, which was the equivalent to Delta Force, he learned an undiscovered talent: killing. He instantly mastered every technique available to quietly eliminate an opponent. He realized that he was especially good at up-close techniques. He also realized a frightening feeling; he enjoyed the planning and the thrill of the final contact with the prey.

After four years, including a year working with the American Green Beret in the hill country of Viet Nam, his army career ended. He returned to Sicily and spent six months in the cliff top city of Taormina. In this beautiful city, overlooking the blue Sea beaches and port below it, he reconnected with his family and made peace.

He and his father daily walked the narrow streets of Taormina, where cars were forbidden. They smiled at the street vendors, sampled the wares of the day, and shook hands with the merchants they were paid to protect. The smells of fresh baked goods, noon specialties in preparation and fresh fruits permeated the air. The varied colors of new knock-off purses, shawls, vests and leather goods displayed on the streets presented a colorful site. The non-stop chatter of the vendors attempting to seduce a tourist created a festive atmosphere. The cool ocean breeze and its salty smell provided a fresh and arousing sensation.

He and his father talked for hours of their heritage and family business. Each day at noon they ate and drank local wine at various small outdoor restaurants overlooking the white-capped sea. Eventfully, they began discussing Arturo's new business and refined its operating guidelines.

Each day after at least a two hour lunch, his father retired to his Villa located at the base of the Castello Mountain area, overlooking Taormina. Arturo would then pursue his favorite hobby: finding, and flirting with a beauty and eventually inducing her to have sex with him for a few torrid hours in his apartment overlooking the cliffs and crashing waves.

Like everything in his life, he pursued this hobby with unlimited pre-planning, calculation and enthusiasm. He discovered a truth about himself; the hunt was more fun than the kill. He never lasted in any relationship as he never felt love, just lust. After a week or two of romance and unrelenting sex, he would find himself bored and ready for a new conquest.

Many a maid in Taormina both hated and loved their brief passionate adventure with the small, handsome, dark-skinned stranger from Palermo, whose wiry body had taught them a great deal about various sexual pleasures. He also taught them that men with money, charm and good looks are not to be trusted.

His new venture, initially financed by his father, was an instant success. It was very simple. Rich people will pay a great deal for justice when they perceive they have been wronged and the court or police system has failed them. Arturo's approach was simple. He took a large down-payment, routed to various Cayman accounts, to research the assignment. This process could take months as the client had to submit all their information to a secret mail drop in Paris, Berlin, or London. He would then, with his father's resources, verify and expand on these facts and allegations. He rejected at least 75% of the requests as simply an irrational claim for revenge and returned 50% of the fee.

When he accepted a case, he spent months planning the process. It involved bribes, spies, and personal observation. No detail went unconsidered. He became a perfectionist at the art of being a vigilante for hire.

He loved the process. He became increasingly adept at making the kill look like an accident. This avoided any problems from the police and a revenge seeking family or business associate. His pleasure at watching a truly bad person receive justice increased each time he delivered it close up. The flood of emotions scared and thrilled him.

After two decades and earning 30 million dollars in fees, his residence in Europe was becoming too risky. Despite protest from his family, he moved to the United States and became a vagabond vigilante. At each stay in New York, Phoenix, Seattle, Chicago, and Kansas City, he practiced his hobby of flirtation and seduction while perfecting his skills at death without detection.

At the age of 55, he was tiring and concerned that his luck might run out. He knew his attention to detail and planning had served him well. He had no pangs of guilt for the victims. They were judged by him as bad people. But the number of governmental law enforcement groups that suspected his existence was increasing along with the number of copy-cat killers. He suspected that he would become the target of his own profession. It was time to disappear.

With a few well-placed bribes, a new identity was born. Doug Valli had a birth certificate from Columbus, Ohio, tax records for 38 consecutive years, a passport, a military record, and a long-term resume as a government employee specializing in agricultural expansion. For a few more dollars, he received multiple degrees from the prestigious agricultural department at Iowa State University and academic credit for a series of publications, displaying his authorship on a broad array of cutting edge agricultural topics.

On a trip to Ames, Iowa, to finalize the records regarding his degrees and academic work, he flew into Des Moines International Airport and was trapped in the middle of a 30 inch blizzard. During his three-day involuntary stay, he explored the town.

The greater Des Moines area had a population of over a half million people. It was built in a tree filled rolling area in the middle of the state. Multiple rivers and streams traversed it landscape. Because of foresighted business leaders, it had a progressive downtown area complete with a boutique-lined skywalk system, and a multi-function arena featuring various acclaimed musical and athletic events. The city had a nationally acclaimed civic center with access to recent Broadway plays and performances. Its annual art festival was nationally rated in the top ten. It had a development league basketball time affiliated with the Phoenix Suns, a Triple A baseball team affiliated with the Chicago Cubs, and an Arena Football team that had been the starting venue for future Hall of Fame quarterback, Kurt Warner.

His brief visit to the Des Moines Art Center made it obvious that it was a world class art museum. He knew that the Drake Relays was a prominent national track and field event and was always nationally televised. Shopping options had grown, particularly on the West Des Moines side of the town which had attracted nationally know shops and restaurants to the Jordan Creek Mall and West Glen Center. There were numerous high quality niche restaurants and a great spa at the West Glen Center. He had enjoyed a deep massage and facial during the later part of the blizzard.

He discovered that Des Moines boosted more insurance industry home offices than any other city. They provided many good paying jobs. As a result many country girls came to the city for a job, to find a man or break their bonds from small town life. The number of these young charming ladies was very interesting to Valli. They were generally naïve, well-educated and refreshingly innocent. Unfortunately, the corn-fed upbringing often brought baggage in the form of 10 pounds of extra weight. He knew he could find ways to encourage the loss of that extra girth.

Most importantly to Valli's decision was the nature of the populace. They were genuine, friendly, accommodating, well-educated, and not overly-inquisitive or suspicious. After his short trip to Ames to complete his bogus degrees and articles, he made a decision. He selected Des Moines as his hiding place.

CHAPTER THREE

"I'm Not Saying My Golf Game Went Bad, But If I Grew Tomatoes They'd Come Up Sliced."

LEE TREVINO

✱✱✱✱✱

THE RETURN TO Des Moines and his lusting thoughts of an evening with 25 year old Mindy Browski eliminated the jet lag. His arrival with the gift of a shawl and pearl necklace was greeted with his favorite dinner, lasagna smothered in bologna sauce, a fresh tossed salad with his own balsamic vinegar dressing, and sex with his gorgeous young woman. Mindy had it all: looks, wit, intelligence, and an aggressive libido. As a bonus, she could cook as well as she could screw, which was next to magnificent.

Seven years after he settled in Des Moines, he met this small town beauty at the nationally acclaimed Des Moines Summer Art Fair. She had just moved to town to take a job with Principal Life Insurance Company, one of the city's largest employers. He had just finished wandering about the Pappajohn Sculpture Park which was the venue of the Art Fair. The Plensa Sculpture was intriguing. One could imagine varied themes being expressed. Art isn't always conveying a message, sometimes it's just art.

He was looking at a unique piece of perpetual motion steel and copper art created by Andrew Carson when he noticed the tall slender dark haired young lady. She was leading a group of senior citizens through the maze of unusual and very expensive art. As she approached, she tripped over a booth's anchor ropes. He swooped in to save her from a rough fall.

After that act of gallantry, he joined the group and charmed the blue haired ladies with his art knowledge and repartee with the vendors. After Mindy put her wards back on the bus, they left the Art Fair to have a late lunch at the reflecting pool at the Art Center. He then commenced his plan for her seduction; a glass of wine, a lot of questions, a few jokes, and a few well placed compliments on her appearance and demeanor. His male bullshit dispenser was operating at a magnum force level.

In a matter of two dates, he achieved his goal of getting her into bed. That moment of animal lust was perfect, but her soft touches and young zest surprised him. He had a strange sensation. He enjoyed her as a person. He further surprised himself as he kept coming back with more reasons to spend time with her. They explored his adopted state like little children absorbing a new subject. After two months, he realized she had lasted a month longer than any other relationship. She made him feel young even when they weren't in bed.

Early in July her enthusiasm surprised him. She jumped at the chance to go with him and his five golf cronies on RAGBRAI. The Register's Annual Great Bike Ride Across Iowa was an unusual and grueling event. Over 22,000 bikers rode from the Missouri River side of Iowa to the Mississippi River side: coast to coast. This annual week-long 400 hundred mile trek was exhausting. It was filled with multiple experiences. For some a family reunion event, for some a health challenge, for some a continual party, and for some it was an opportunity for cheating on a spouse or reconnecting with special friend with benefits.

The six aging golf buddies formed Team Grey Goose. The stated goal was to get in shape and enjoy the fun of this unique experience. They were bored with their post-retirement lives. It was too repetitive. Get up. Watch the stock market. Have breakfast. Play a mediocre round of golf. Have a few drinks. Have dinner. Lie about their successful and interesting sex lives. Do it all over again the next day. They wanted something new, especially if it presented a chance to flirt with and maybe seduce attractive physically fit female participants.

Valli looked forward to having Mindy by his side. The other five looked forward to vigorously exploring the rumors and legends about the sexual promiscuity associated with this trip. In the end, despite their undaunted efforts, they reluctantly concluded that 60 year old men with lots of money, charm, and unlimited lines of macho BS, have virtually no chance to find quick sex with a younger woman. The free love attitude of the 70's had few survivors still riding on this trip, and the survivors looked very old to them. All five knew they didn't really look their age.

Mindy had been a trooper; always ready for the next day, tolerant of his time with the sexually frustrated five some, and on a moment's notice ready to snuggle in the rear of the RV with her old trophy. The trip had ended on a weird note.

The team organizer, Lee Scott, had recently lost two previously intimate female friends from a prior RAGBRAI ride to unexpected heart attacks. At one funeral, he heard other similar deaths. By illegally accessing Polk County records, the overly curious group had concluded several other women in the area had similar deaths over the past few years. They did not believe in coincidences.

Scott knew his dead acquaintances had all loved to workout and be pampered at expensive spas. Through illegally entering into the computer records of several spa and health clubs facilities, they found the common thread: one spa where all victims were regular members. Breaking into that spa and accessing its records by bypassing all security systems was easy. They isolated two massage therapists who were regular participants in RAGBRAI during their vacations. The deceased ladies had all enjoyed their massages.

By breaking enough laws to earn them each 100 years in prison, the amateur detectives then assembled convincing proof of their guilt as serial killers. Everywhere the two moved, healthy wealthy women who enjoyed spa services died. The illegal break in of their home, where they found the trophies from their kills were found, was conclusive.

After completing the grueling trip, the geriatric vigilante struggled with alternatives as to what to do with this situation. They found one of their group, Matt Fielding, was intimately involved with one of the suspects. As they pondered how to handle this issue, luck stepped in. One of the two killed his partner over the rights to kill Fielding, the next victim.

While the remaining killer was illegally interrogated after being kidnapped, a funny thing happened. After admitting everything, Roy Roses, serial killer of over 20 women, simply dropped dead. The stress of his interrogation appeared to be the cause. Only Scott, the team's self-proclaimed organizer, motivator and center of knowledge of all worldly matters, suspected Valli was at work. The almond smell of cyanide was a solid clue. Valli's wink of confirmation was the clincher.

After some remorse and much debate, the decision was made. Why take up the time of the packed judicial system? Roy was quickly disposed of in a vat of extremely destructive newly invented chemical stored in Fielding's warehouse. In 30 minutes, Roy was on a happy trail to where ever serial killers go for an eternity. No body legally means no crime.

Team Grey Goose members knew the result was just. The legal system could have never convicted the pair. All the evidence was illegally obtained. The six would likely serve time for their crimes, committed solely in the name of justice. They vowed to leave the subject behind to never again be discussed. Besides, they rationalized that the Iowa prison system was too crowded. They, in fact, had done the State's penal system a service.

Mindy never knew of these events. She thought Valli was a retired agricultural consultant who retired to the quiet life of Des Moines, playing golf to an excess and enjoying his golden years. She did not know his dark side. Few people did.

She didn't know that while he did plan on retiring, the thrill of delivering one more act of justice nagged at him daily. Aging without new experiences is for the infirmed, the mindless and the lazy.

THE SKIES WERE FULL OF DUCKS AND GEESE forming their flocks for the 2011 migration. They were part of the fall sounds in the Midwest. It was a beautiful October day at Glen Oaks Country Club. The leaves were turning to multiple colors, the breeze only five miles an hour, and the air crisp. It was good to be alive.

Valli's partner, Scott, as usual was the source of constant competitive barbs. This came very naturally to an overly-aggressive, semi-retired lawyer with diminishing golf skills. They were two holes behind with two holes to go. A 100 dollars was about to go into Fielding's and his partner Snyder's pockets unless the difficult finishing two par fours were won.

Scott taunted, "Snyder, I don't care how good of an athlete you were at Stanford. You are about to suffer defeat. Put that computer geek mind of yours to work and figure out how to avoid imminent disaster. Valli and I have just discovered the swing of swings."

With a laugh Snyder returned the jab. "Stop with the lawyer lame tricks, Scott. You two are toast. I have seen the way your once smooth putting stroke has become a yipping stab"

Snyder stepped to the tee of the difficult 410 yard par four seventeenth. It had fescue in front of the tee, a tree lined creek on the right, and a lake in front protecting the green. His six foot lean frame oozed of athletic talent. His shoulder length gray hair made him look like a cover model for AARP magazine. With a long sweeping effort, his appearance of grandeur disappeared into the reality of being a golf hack. The ball rolled 100 yards off the tee into a deep fescue covered area. Scott turned to make a futile effort at concealing his laugh.

"That 300 yard second shot over water could be a challenge," Scott said to Snyder with a feeble effort at sounding sincere.

Snyder had been a state basketball hero in the early 60's and had gone to Stanford. After a couple of seasons, he lost interest in basketball and focused on the fast developing computer and internet business. He associated with some of its early pioneers. However his propensity for chasing young co-eds diverted him from making the billions these early geeks later amassed. He had done very well financially by developing several internet businesses and selling them at their peak. Half of his fortunes had been lost by three divorces all caused by his wanderlust.

Fielding was shaken by the melt-down of his partner. He pushed his drive to the right into a deep wooded ravine paralleling that side of the fairway. He scratched his hatless head. His thinning curly hair was in disarray. He looked like an aging Al Franken squinting through his small professorial glasses at a disaster in the making.

Scott and Valli each hit mediocre but straight shots. Their bogies held up, and they won. The 18th tee box was theirs. To the victors goes the tee. With the swagger of bullfighters, they each took their best swings and each drove the ball into the deep fescue grass on the right where an ancient decaying tree blocked the next shot to the green.

Snyder and Fielding drove their shots half-way up the steep hilly fairway. They followed these acts of perceived skill with long iron shots deep into the bunker on the right side of the green. Fielding's sand shot hit near the pin located on the front right of the green and rolled down the hill over thirty yards. Snyder skulled his sand shot, and it was last seen heading west into the fairway of the 17th hole.

Team Scott and Valli chipped out of the fescue with swings that resembled lumbermen chopping trees. Fescue flew in abundance. They hit their next shot to the green and prevailed with double bogies. Both gingerly used three putts to accomplish this awesome task.

With the typical grace that exemplified this gentlemen's game, Snyder mumbled. "Your turn to buy even if we did tie, you greasy grungy piece of dog crap."

Golf games involving aging talent deficient males should always end in a tie. No one deserves to win. The four went quietly to the posh bar overlooking the eighteenth green. Admitting that you were a golf hack is a sobering experience for proud males.

The newly decorated club house, pro shop, and large bar were classy and fresh. The three new owners had bought the club out of bankruptcy at a good price. Ron Pearson, retired president of Hy-Vee Stores, Robert Pulver, a very prominent local business man, and Mark Oman, a successful Wells Fargo banker, had stepped up, taken a risk, and saved the club from becoming a public golf club. They used their business skills and mapped a clear new course for the operations. They executed their vision flawlessly and invested wisely. They had given the tired facility a face-lift, a clear direction and an image of permanency. Membership was revitalized!

The four golf warriors entered the bar overlooking both the tenth and eighteenth holes attempting to forget the past four hours of mental torture through the magic of liquor. It was full and the atmosphere upbeat. This was the image the founding owners had hoped for 15 years before when they over built the club during the biggest summer rains in Iowa history.

After the normal exchange of jabs and insults, the cold beers arrived. Scott held his frosty mug high. "To friends, competitors, and pals! May we live forever to tell the world about our many feminine conquests."

Everyone laughed and clicked mugs.

Snyder sighed. "I don't know about you but those female conquests are getting few and far between. I know I have been rejected by every lady in a 50 mile radius who is within 10 years of my age. I think word is getting around that I am a shallow, self-absorbed womanizer. I don't remember why I ever worried about what to do if an erection lasted more than four hours?"

Scott grinned over his beer mug. "How would an unfounded rumor like your being a callous self absorbed womanizer ever get started? Maybe you need to emphasize that gangster roll in your left pocket to impress any young admirer?"

Snyder paused, "If only I had stayed with that bunch of computer geeks in California instead of trying to commit suicide by screwing. I would be in some exotic location being pampered by a bevy of young women instead of suffering the abuse of a bunch of toothless lions in the wasteland of Iowa."

Scott ordered another round. "We need to talk about our friend Tim O'Brien. Have you guys noticed anything weird with his behavior?"

Scott had a very soft side. His macho talk covered an unhealed wound from the loss of his wife and soulmate to the Big C four years prior.

His gaze became serious. "I am very concerned. Tim was scheduled to play today as we can now play as a five-some. I called his condo at the Plaza. I received no answer, so I called security. They said he went for a walk early this morning and hasn't returned. Have any of you noticed some bizarre behavior?"

Fielding leaned back in his chair and scratched his always disheveled hair. "I noticed last week he kept calling me Lucas. It is hard to confuse us. He is six foot six and 250 pounds and likes women. I am five foot eight and 180 pounds and like men. Of course, we are both strikingly handsome. I just passed it off, as periodically he would call me Matt, Fielding or Ass-Hole. I did notice last week at Des Moines Golf, he was starting to hit toward number 18th green when we were on the 13th tee box. I just thought he was kidding."

Valli frowned. "I wasn't going to mention it, but last week, when Mindy had you old farts over for dinner, he introduced himself and said glad to meet you when she opened the door. She just blew it off, but later mentioned that he looked confused."

The room was silent. Aging people have little moments where their mental computer skips. They fear that moment when it's not temporary, but a real systems crash.

"I have known him a long time. He developed multiple transportation schemes for some very big companies. He made a fortune cutting their warehousing and transportation costs. He raised two children after his wife, Carol, ran off with the soccer coach. He was anal in keeping track of details. This worries me," Scott said.

Valli ordered another round. "When Fielding developed his latest invention the logistics of getting it manufactured and distributed were mind boggling. Tim handled it flawlessly without even a note. He did the same thing when Mindy took over the marketing for our little cubby fag friend. I'm concerned."

Fielding, while laughing at Valli's politically incorrect comment, choked on his beer. "I will forgive your lack of tact in referring to me as a fag as part of your typical male insensitivity, you wrinkled, shriveled-up little molester of young girls. By the way has Mindy seen the light and decided to dump your sorry old ass yet?" The two clicked mugs and laughed.

Snyder leaned forward deep in thought. "You know, when we did that bike ride from Carroll to Perry last week, Tim acted weird when we were at the Templeton Rye operation in Templeton. When the tour guide was explaining how it was developed in the prohibition days to supplement farmer's meager income, and how its major marketer, Al Capone, referred to it as "The Good Stuff," Tim looked totally blank. He later asked me who was this Capone guy, why he bought all this brown stuff, and why we stopped at a pizza place. I just thought he was acting goofy and laughed. Scott, while you were trying to get a case of their small batch nectar of the gods, he was outside watching down the road. Nothing was moving or happening where he was looking."

Snyder finished his beer and ordered each a shot of Templeton Rye. "Those two Iowa boys had one great idea restarting the Templeton Rye operation. Scott Bush with the MIT education and finance background, and Keith Kerkhoff, a local Buena Vista University football hero, with a talent for production, with the family recipe, make a great partnership. My only regret is I can't buy it by the case. It is The Good Stuff!"

Scott downed his shot. "Why don't you all come over Saturday? We can watch Iowa screw up and lose to Northwestern in the last few minutes, cook a steak and consume some more adult beverages. I will make sure Tim is there and we can watch what unravels. Let's say three o'clock at the Scott Sugar Shack. If anyone has a date, which I assume is unlikely, bring her or him along."

Four aging friends gave each other a nod of approval, a hand slap and left. Everyone had a nagging feeling about Tim and a pang of fear about themselves. The worry of mental decay lurks deep within the dark corners of all aging minds. When seen up close and real, it is paralyzing. Scott walked to his car. Tears fell from his deep brown eyes. He recalled all the times he had corrected Tim's club selection. Tim, use the putter not the driver. Use the wedge not the wood!

Valli sat in the plush seat of his new Mercedes coupe. He was frozen looking at the sunset. His mind drifted to Mindy. Every time something happened, he wanted to share it with her while he was still young enough to keep her. Was that love or just the selfishness of an aging man?

Snyder sat in front of his locker and shook his head. He did an unusual thing. He dialed a lady friend his own age and asked her to dinner. He did not feel like being alone.

Fielding lowered his head to the steering wheel and cried uncontrollably. Tears filled his glasses and poured down his rosy round cheeks.

CHAPTER FOUR

"I Arise In The Morning Torn Between A Desire To Improve The World And A Desire To Enjoy The World. This Makes It Hard To Plan The Day."

E.B. WHITE

✳✳✳✳✳

THE EVENING WAS turning from a beautiful fall day to a blustery wet night. A small red haired man entered The Plaza condominiums on Third and Locust. The security guard of the fifteen floor luxury condo building was taken aback. The man looked like a drowned rat as he looked at the elevator entrance.

"Mr. O'Brien are you okay? Can I help you?"

"Thanks, I guess I left my keys in my unit. Can you help me?"

The large retired policeman quickly ushered O'Brien to the elevator and punched the pent house button. "We need to get you inside and dried off. Did you get caught outside without an umbrella or coat?"

"Ya, that's it. I went for a walk and this storm slipped in on me."

Guard Forest Norvell looked long at the bedraggled small aging man. The storm had been going on for five hours. He took Tim O'Brien under his large arm and guided him to his penthouse.

O'Brien dried off after a hot shower. He poured himself a full glass of The Good Stuff and looked out the expansive east window bank. He owned all four units on the top floor and had a view of the city from every direction. He was now focused on the golden dome of the Capitol Building which stood a few blocks away. He shivered, not from the cold, but from fear. He could not recall where he had been, how he got back and how he got wet.

He was frozen by a growing fear. He did know what was happening. These episodes of blanking out and losing track of times were recurring. He had embarrassed himself too many times in front of his dear friends. He slipped into a trance in the middle of that thought.

THE SUN WAS COMING UP. Its bright rays through the dissipating storm clouds sent heat onto O'Brien's face. He awoke with a start. He was again soaked. Mud was all over the walnut floor. He looked at the clock. It was eight in the morning.

O'Brien remembered feeling the sensation of a strong wind in his face as he drove through the downtown like a driver at the Des Moines Grand Prix. He walked out to the elevator and went to the basement. His restored 320i BMW convertible stood in its normal stall. Its sleek red metal was covered with mud. The front left bumper was smashed and rubbing against the tire. There was blood on the grill. He held his breath. Where had he been? What had he done?

As he approached the convertible he noticed a matted mess in the back seat. He was paralyzed. He expected a human body but found a very maimed and stiff whitetail deer carcass. He put it in a large trash bag and dropped it in the trash bin. Hope the pick-up comes before tomorrow he thought.

O'Brien leaned against his car and erupted into laughter. He hadn't killed anyone. The laugh quickly turned to sobs. His episodes were getting longer and more frequent, and the moments of clarity shorter. He rushed back to his unit. He was nearing a panic attack. What is happening?

After a long hot shower, he sat looking south over the Principal Ball Park which was home for the Triple A Iowa Cubs. He sat at his breakfast table slowly sipping a cup of pressed coffee. He turned east to look at the beauty of the fall sunrise over the Capitol.

His gaze fixed on the adjacent wall and the three Sarah Grant paintings that made the wall a statement. Looking at the pieces entitled "I Finally See Myself Again." "Pull Back the Curtain," and "My Favorite Year to Come Home" as usual brought a smile to his face. His hands unconsciously moved over the carvings on The Sticks table that Sarah had designed and personalized to display his favorite events, people and sayings. His hands stopped and gently rubbed the names of his children and the saying, "Children are Everything."

Sarah Grant has become one of Iowa's most famous artists. Her art is proudly displayed in numerous state buildings, university buildings, charitable facilities and the entrances to Iowa's largest employers. The Mural "What I Love about Iowa" was created for the State's sesquicentennial celebration. Sticks, Inc sells nationally unique and personalized furniture and accessories through over 100 outlets.

O'Brien was slipping into a haze when a knock at the door interrupted him and snapped his mind back to the moment. He opened the door and for a moment did not recognize the nattily dressed, smiling, stout man with salt and pepper hair who, without a welcome, entered his home. Scott gave him a bear hug.

Scott released his long hug. "I am here to take you to the "Scott Sugar Shack" for the Iowa football game, good fun, excessive drinking, and my own home cooked swordfish encrusted in almonds and coconut. Are you ready?"

"Scott, why did you stop? Were you afraid I would get lost or forget to come?" O'Brien reacted in an angry flash of emotion.

"No Tim. I was just downtown at Woody's Smoke Shack getting his amazing ribs, brisket and cornbread with honey. I got an extra pan of cornbread for you. I remembered it was one of your addictions. I just stopped up to deliver it. I hoped I would interrupt you having outrageously dirty sex with one of the young 50 year olds you brag about."

O'Brien regained his composure, and his long term memory kicked in. "Thanks for the cornbread. Woody and Cheryl Wasson have come a long way since his construction days. A bad construction economy drove him to convert a hobby into a business. I remember years ago when he was winning all of those barbeque event prizes. I can never pass his place on Cottage Grove without stopping and ordering something. The homemade cherry pies are also addictive."

Scott was taken aback by his recall. He smiled.

O'Brien picked up a large slice of cornbread and generously coated it with honey. He took a huge bite and smiled. "Thanks for stopping. You are a good friend. I will follow you on my motorcycle."

He remembered the deer mess in his back seat.

IOWA LOST BY TWO POINTS. Northwestern maintained its curse of the Hawkeyes. Everyone was depressed, bored, and pissed. It is tough to be a Hawkeye fan.

"Too bad Walz couldn't be here to watch the Hawks fuck up another close game. When is he coming back from Washington?" asked Snyder as he sipped his drink.

Scott looked up as he prepared the almond coating on the swordfish.

"I talked to him last week. He is likely to stay another six months. His original assignment was to work out a testing protocol and related methods to determine if applicants had the mental strength to act as drone pilots. As he explained, these people spend hours sitting in an air-conditioned room in various sites in the United States or allied countries. They fly drones over many unfriendly countries at very high altitudes. Their cameras, listening devices, and sensor equipment provide incredible detail and intelligences. However, the stress of long hours can be nerve-racking. When that stress is combined with the potential for killing someone with their little rockets, the potential of a mental breakdown or error has dire consequences"

"Walz's work has progressed beyond tests on new applicants. He is now developing testing methods to determine the long term capacity of veteran pilots for handling the built up stress. He wants to stay and apply his tests to the entire group to determine if someone in the current ranks is about to become a kamikaze drone pilot. Walz is a genius at creating various forms of stress and then testing the results."

Scott laughed. "He is learning to fly the drones himself. He has crashed two so far. They only trust him with the old propeller driven jobs that are nearly worn out. His piloting skills must be on the same level as his golf skills."

"I think he feels good about doing something productive. He has a drawer full of Viet Nam medals, and he has never lost that military pride. He says he misses these golden years' frivolous times, but he has a renewed sense of value. I guess we all need that feeling. Here's a salute to Lucas Walz, patriot, friend, and the worst putter in the state." Scott downed his drink and returned to his culinary task with vengeance.

Everyone noticed O'Brien looking out the window. The prairie below was golden as the sunset colored the drying prairie grass and wild flowers. Several deer wandered by mindlessly grazing in the fading sun.

"Tim, what have you been up to?" asked Snyder as he moved over to the sad little figure and put his arm on his shoulder.

"I was just enjoying the view and thinking how much of this I have taken for granted. It's absorbing and very calming. I will miss it. And you guys."

"What do you plan on doing? Running off with that lady you keep talking about, Connie Whatsherface?"

Tim broke from his staring at the prairie. "We broke up. She was 54, wealthy, attractive and professed to like my fading sexual efforts. She was getting too serious. I realized that I am just a terrible catch for any woman, no matter what her age. I am too selfish to care what she thinks or feels, and too lazy to want to get to know their friends or family. Besides, I am planning a long trip. I need a change. I will let you know the details when I have them worked out."

Valli was in an unusually light mood. He toasted to everyone, their friendship, and his Mindy. There, in front of all, he handed her a ring that would allow an early retirement for our jeweler friend, Carroll Devode. Valli, with a sudden mood of seriousness, fell to one knee in front of Mindy and reached for her hand.

"May we always be friends, lovers, and soulmates. Will you marry this aging old guy who for the first time has found love?"

Mindy cried. His words were good for a man still trying to get in touch with his feelings. But, clearly he did not have a role as a romantic lover in the cinema.

Scott brushed a tear away and raised his fresh glass to toast the new couple. "To my aging good friend and his beautiful lady. May she love him in his walker and depends in 20 years as much as she does now."

Templeton Rye splashed from the click of glasses.

CHAPTER FIVE

"Friendship With Ones Self Is All Important, Because Without It One Cannot Be Friends With Anyone Else In The World."

ELEANOR ROOSEVELT

✳✳✳✳✳

THE JANUARY SUN WAS SETTING IN THE WEST. The Mazatzal Mountains on the east side of the Ranch Course at Tonto Verde Arizona were fast becoming a radiant pink color.

Scott took out his driver and looked at the 500 yard par five 17th hole. Desert to the left, desert to the right, and a large trap in the middle were the only obstacles to overcome with the drive. "Just two more holes to go and we can observe the local slogan: 'When the mountains turn pink, it's time to drink.'"

Scott hit a good drive to the right of the trap. It set up the second shot over another arroyo. If the second shot was properly executed, it would set up the third shot with a short iron over another arroyo to a heavily bunkered green. Isn't golf a simple game?

Walz slowly moved his huge frame to the tee. His Viet Nam-damaged hip was clearly causing him pain.

"I think the days of playing 36 holes are in the rear view mirror for me, guys. We have three more days in the Valley of the Sun and I suggest we pace ourselves. We are all in our 60s, if that has slipped your degenerating old minds. Okay, Scott, you just set a good example as I intend to make you look wimpy with this drive. We can win this one and you two old farts are buying dinner."

Waltz put his entire 250 pound frame into the swing. The ball was launched like a bullet. Unfortunately, it was a misguided bullet. It came to rest 50 yards deep in the desert to the left of the fairway. He was 200 yards from the green.

"Perfect. I love hitting that next shot. I only need to find a swing among 100 Staghorn cacti, avoid 20 tall Saguaro cacti, and hit a 200 yard second shot to the green. I see a birdie coming right up."

Fielding habitually scratched his nearly bald head. Hair was pointing in every direction. He turned to his partner. "It looks like a big opportunity has come our way, Valli. We both know Scott can never hit three good shots in a row, and Walz will look like a porcupine when he gets out of the desert."

With that bit of false bravado, Fielding hit a drive down the middle three feet short of the trap directly in the center of the fairway.

Valli followed suit. He yelled, "Where are we going to dinner tonight Fielding? Make it expensive. How about Maestros? I love their 16 ounce rib eye steak, lobster mashed potatoes, and expensive French wine."

Much to their shock, Scott hit a second good ball and was only 100 yards from the green. He was in perfect shape. He just had to hit uphill over one more arroyo and avoid the trap to the right front and the one behind the green. No challenge for a 16 handicap golfer who still believed he was a single digit player.

Walz hit a monster shot out of the desert which buried itself pin high in the trap to the south side of the undulating green. He limped out of the desert picking Staghorn thorns from his left hand, arm, and hip.

Valli and Fielding hit two good shots to the green, and were trying not to laugh as Scott choked and bladed his wedge over the green into the trap where Walz's ball was plugged. After three swings each, the two deflated warriors of the fairways, Scott and Walz, picked their balls up and admitted that they were ready for the 18th hole, which would be quickly followed by a couple of stiff drinks. The victors turned their backs to shield their laugher and smirks. Even when they know it, it's never good to laugh at a friend's ineptitude.

Hole 18 ended in a tie. The mountains were pink and the exhausted foursome sped to the clubhouse to start cocktail hour. It was time to sedate their aching muscles and crushed athletic images. They sat on the veranda of the Tonto Verde Country Club watching the deep pink shades of the mountains to the east fade as the sun sank in the west. The pond below them was deep blue and mirror calm, except for periodic schools of small fish enjoying their evening feeding.

Scott held his second glass of Grey Goose Vodka high over his head. "Here is to Snyder whose illness kept him home, and to Tim O'Brien, who is gone but will always be with us in spirit."

All four took a deep swallow and became quiet. Walz broke the silence. "I guess I understand that Tim ended his life last month. He must have known something was going very wrong with his mind and finished it while he could. What a sight he must have been pedaling in the night to the Trestle Bridge. We must have biked over it 10 times this year so it was vivid in his mind."

Scott nodded and wiped a tear away.

"I usually don't condone ending life that way. It leaves a lot of emotion and messes for those who are left behind. I do understand it this time. His affairs were in perfect order. All his eight million dollars in assets were in trusts for his three kids and their heirs. Even his note to us was precise; Live life to its fullest, follow new dreams and never look back. I will be watching as the next chapters are written."

As they sat quietly watching the dusk descend, the pink on the mountains fade, and listening to the coyotes howl as their packs formed for a night hunt, they were startled. Snyder's tall lanky frame entered the veranda with a serving-tray filled with another round of drinks. His mane of white shoulder length hair was perfectly coifed around his bronze lean facial features.

"What a sorry bunch of old woman-chasing hulks you four look like."

Fielding jumped up to help Snyder with the slopping drinks. "Careful, an ounce of liquor is like an erection. Never waste one. I thought you were home recovering from the robotic prostrate surgery?"

"I couldn't stay home even if golf is off-limits for a few weeks. I caught a ride down from a friend of mine on his new jet. I renewed our friendship last fall at Glen Oaks. He is one of the owners. I may move there."

"I couldn't stand not being part of our annual get-ready for-winter trip. Besides, I figures on winning enough at gin to pay for the dinner I intend to buy you all tonight. Not to mention one of my new computer schemes just sold for enough to cover my last divorce. If my prostrate surgery didn't damage the erection creating nerve, I can chase young women with an even larger budget in my pocket."

Scott laughed, "When will you know if all is well with all the equipment of your old unit?"

Snyder took a deep sip. "A couple of months from now I can go for a solo and check it all out. I am deciding if I work on finding a young lady who feels a need to participate in my medical experiments, or just fly to Vegas, rent a car and head to the Bunny Ranch for expert assistance."

"Buying experience is more predictable. I am not sure that your white mane of hair, will attach anything but a blue-hair. But, maybe Mindy has a young friend who has a limited I.Q who would enjoy you for a few hours," Valli chuckled.

AFTER THREE MORE DAYS of mediocre golf, great food, and too much booze, the five sat exhausted and quiet in the corner of the Tonto Verde Club House. The evening trips to local pick-up bars ended after the first two evenings with no success. A big cup of corn chowder and a plate of the featured bison burger meatloaf topped with garlic whipped potatoes had been consumed by each of them. They were exhausted.

Scott quietly reflected. "It just doesn't seem right to be going back and knowing Tim is gone. I know Valli has a wedding to plan, but personally, I am nearing total boredom. I have a few legal projects, but they aren't exciting. I have to find a new trail to follow. What are you guys going to do?"

Walz slid back. "I am going to Nevada and then North Dakota. I want to keep working on revising my tests to determine when stress is about to make one of those drone pilots goofy. It has been exciting working with those young joystick heroes. It is amazing what they can see, hear, and do with those little marvels. It's the Air Force of the future. I have even convinced them to let me keep training after I wrecked two more old ones on landing. They were old and obsolete anyway."

"I envy your enthusiasm, Lucas. Are you into the flying hummingbird drones yet?" Scott asked.

"As a matter of fact, I am. I can't tell you anything beyond what was in Time Magazine and some other newspapers, but they are something else. They look like hummingbirds. They transmit what they see and hear, and they can get very close to their target. I have wrecked a flock so far, but those kids operate them like just another video game. Careful what you say, one of them could be hiding in a tree or hovering over you at anytime. They are the answer to controlling our border."

The evening eventually returned to the suicide of O'Brien.

Walz said, "I have been around a lot of stress and potential suicide situations. In Viet Nam I saw it happen to young guys who were confused, scared, and constantly unnerved. It is always a possibility from the tests and failures that I work with. I always preach that suicide is a very selfish act. It leaves someone else to clean up the mess. It leaves loved ones confused and even guilty. But, maybe I understand here."

Snyder in an unusually sober mood said, "Alzheimer Disease is something I fear every day. Every time I forget a name, every time I forget the time for a meeting, and every time I forget what I was saying in mid sentence, I cringe. How about you guys?"

Scott paused, "I am doing a lot of reading. Some experts feel we need to get over the idea that we are committed to aging with diminished memories and mind function. They feel a lot of our failures are a matter of lack of concentration and falling victim to accepting a self- fulfilling prophesy. New mental challenges, physical conditioning, and a young attitude appear to be the recommended treatment. Some studies even show that diminished mental capacity can be stabilized with mental development games. I am looking into going to a Des Moines female doctor who recently got a degree in anti-aging medicine. Human growth hormones may be added to my evening cocktails in the future. Besides, I hear she is cute. I wonder how complete her physical will be?"

Snyder said, "If she is very complete in her check-up of your body and history, she may reject you as a project that could ruin her reputation."

Valli leaned forward. "I understand Tim's note about looking for new dreams and never looking back. I may be doing one more of my specialized consulting gigs before the marriage. I just can't get the feeling of a great adrenalin rush out of my system. I may need some expert help from discrete eyes in the sky, an inventor, a computer nerd, and a bossy general know it all part- time lawyer. Are you interested?"

All were silent and then nodded.

Valli asked, "What if I told you that we will violate as many laws as we did last summer eliminating the RAGBRAI killers? This time we are looking at avoiding a merger between a hillbilly pot dealer's empire and a Mexican cartel.

Scott smiled nodded and held up his glass. "Here is to Tim O'Brien. May he be the angel on our shoulder?"

CHAPTER SIX

"Getting Married For Sex Is Like Buying A 747 For The Peanuts."

JEFF FOXWORTHY

*****

THE WEDDING PLANNING was progressing as smoothly as such a traumatic event can proceed. To his friend's surprise, Valli was mellow and at ease while Mindy's female anxiety gene surged. She browsed endlessly through bridal magazines, surfed the web for ideas, and constantly reviewed ads from wedding planners. She obsessively exchanged dreams with her married friends. She changed her mind like the winter weather across Iowa. "Big wedding? No, let's go with a small wedding? No, a destination wedding in Bora Bora, Tahiti, or Rome? Shit let's run off?"

Valli and Mindy sat on the overstuffed couch in his bedroom, holding hands and watching the late spring blizzard cover the ground with large moist flakes. They had just finished a light meal of salad and coconut encrusted halibut. The spotlights from the deck adjacent to the wide bay window displayed the heavily treed Water Works Park located immediately below Valli's Condo at Owl's Head. It was quickly being coated with the accumulating snow. The drab brown of the past winter was being erased and replaced by wavy white drifts. The blinking silver orbs from grazing deer eyes flashed in the evening. At least 20 were getting a final nibble of tender spring grass before it was buried in the heavy wet snow.

She slowly sipped her first glass of Travis Peak Port. "I am surprised at the lack of spontaneity from my married girlfriends. They talk of their date nights as programmed events and sex as a duty. I can't imagine ever saying I will have to do my wifely duties tonight; it's Friday. I think they got married too soon to guys who eventually bored them. I can't imagine us becoming bored. Can you?"

He was careful to deliver a well thought out response. "I have never been married, so what do I know about marriage and boredom? Before I met you, the longest I ever lasted with anyone was three weeks. We need to always remember to keep our lives invigorated and varied. Repetitiveness and predictability are words that I don't think are assets in keeping love alive."

She tilted her head and gave her naughty girl look. "By the way, speaking of invigorating, all this planning ended today at Victoria's Secret. I have several different sets of sexy items for your inspection and approval. I also found a porno DVD. I can't figure how anyone but an Olympic gymnast can do that newly acclaimed Floating Butterfly position. Want to help me understand it?"

They locked eyes, kissed, caressed, and moved together to the bed. Not a word was uttered or necessary. Eye contact communicated complete sentences. They slowly entered the bed. It was oversized, stainless steel framed, covered with a black silk spread and filled with multicolored pillows. The designer from Trieste had done a great job. She has a flair for tasteful but unusual. It was very male, very bold and yet not gaudy. Valli by nature would have made it gaudy with too much old world décor and too many masculine statements with bad art and accessories. With the flick of a switch, the fire in the large stone fireplace crackled. Sounds of the wind and blizzard were perfect background music for the passion that sexy blue lacy panties and bra and an instructional porn tape inspired. Valli had to fake passionate cries of pleasure twice when a cramp hit his 69 year old hip muscles while trying to keep up with his partner.

After great sex and a few cuddles, she quickly fell asleep. He was wide awake. He knew his vigorous display of male virility had lasted an hour. He looked at the clock. He was close. It had lasted 15 minutes.

His mind could not forget the newly arrived file from Palermo. How could he consider one more project and put this new relationship at risk? He had never felt this way about anyone. Was it real love or an aging man's fantasy? Time would tell.

In the quiet of the evening, he could feel the urge building inside him. The euphoria of delivering justice to bad people for a price was enticing. He spent some time thinking about his future and new life. He moved to the large aquarium that filled an entire corner of his living room. The water was crystal clear, the bubbling of the aerators was strong, and the water testing devices were all in the green zone. He hit the light button. The occupants came to life with this signal of a feeding.

The dozen colorful fish increased their movement. Except for the Puffer Fish, they rushed to the surface anticipating a feeding. The five-six inch long Puffer Fish were quietly grazing on the bottom waiting for a late evening snack to settle to them. Watching the occupants in the tank had always been relaxing to Valli. Each fish had a vicious side, yet they had learned to live and let live.

Valli broke his gaze at the bubbling tank. He decided to reread the cover sheet and file that lay in a secret compartment in his desk.

" Arturo, this consulting effort involves stopping a merger of a U.S. and a Mexican drug operation. If they combine, their poison will kill and maim many ignorant users. The reward for avoiding the merger and eliminating the leadership is 10 million dollars. A very rich person has lost a daughter to their poison and wants revenge. The judicial system will never deliver justice. It is too compromised and uncreative. This is your biggest boldest effort. Decide if you want one more journey down this path. You are welcome back to Palermo anytime."

He looked at the bed. She was snuggled deep under a mountain of pillows and the goose down comforter. The soft whimper of satisfaction occasionally slipped from her. He knew he would do it. This effort would need considerable planning and some assistance. He knew his four friends were anxious to get going on a new chapter in their lives, but he needed a perfectly crafted plan.

Education: What Is It? How Do I Get It?

****

PART TWO

"I Know A Lot Of People Thinks I Am Dumb. Well, At Least I Ain't No Educated Fool."

LEON SPINKS

CHAPTER SEVEN

"Education Is A Progressive Discovery Of Our Own Ignorance."

WILL DURANT

*****

JESSE LEE MARVIN WAS LIVING proof that you did not have to be educated, good looking or charming to make a lot of money in the United States. He was a small, sloppily dressed, crude speaking man with an eighth-grade education. Jesse, however, was born with boundless energy, an inquisitive mind, an uncanny ability to detect how to make a profit and a sharply-honed survivor's instinct. When these characteristics were combined with a villainous black heart and a complete disregard for other people and the law, he could not help but make a lot of money. He could have been a Baron of Wall Street had he attended Harvard or Yale.

Ironically, without Jesse's conscious awareness, his business development process closely mirrored an MBA level textbook's tutorials for proper business development. However, unlike many creative business icons, he developed great business plans and developed a multi-million dollar business without wasting time in corporate process and ass-covering. He never saw the need for engaging in tedious analytical processes, repeated planning strategy sessions, multiple meetings to evaluate prior meetings and decisions, and endless time and costs seeking the counsel and by-in of others.

By following his intuitive senses, he missed the joys of endless meetings, unlimited back-biting, unrepentant ass-kissing and the pleasures of sucking-up to a superior. He was a true American entrepreneur. Harvard, Yale or Wharton Business's Schools could make his development process a mandatory case study for streamlined success.

He was on a path to becoming a major player in a merger that could spawn drugs throughout the entire Midwest. If it was successful it would be the prototype for other areas.

CHAPTER EIGHT

"Education Is The Path From Cocky Ignorance To Miserable Uncertainty."

M ARK T WAIN

✼✼✼✼✼

In order to form any successful business, the founders need to acquire the fundamental education that will allow them to understand their business's climate and niche, and to allow them to identify how to prosper in an ever-changing environment. Such an education can take varied forms from highly technical education, theoretical classroom education to on the job training.

Jesse was born to a poor, uneducated family near Pisgah, Iowa in Harrison County in 1978. His parents, Sam and Mary, were uneducated share-croppers. They seldom had enough money to feed or properly clothe a family of three boys. Education took a second seat to survival. Sam drank cheap whiskey whenever he could steal it and supplemented the family's needs by occasionally stealing a pig, a calf, or chickens. He always cheated his landlord by miscounting wagons of grain, and was rarely asked to share-crop a farm more than two years in a row. Sam eventually disappeared, one step ahead of the law, when his greed led him to stealing, butchering, and selling meat from a neighbor's prize herd of Angus cattle and selling the prize bulls for breeding stock.

Sam's quick departure taught Jesse a lesson; always have an exit strategy.

Young Jesse learned the art of stealing by assisting his father in the middle of the night herding livestock into a small, rickety trailer, or catching and bagging chickens or turkeys. He also learned the art of selling hot merchandise while he accompanied Sam to meet with customers in their decaying 1960 Ford 150 pick-up. He always sat quietly and listened as his father negotiated the price for the product. He noticed that the buyers often were well dressed and drove nice cars. His father was an expert at using the plight of his family as the reason to sell too cheap.

Jesse recognized a couple of the buyers as local restaurant operators. He also recognized the buyer of the prize Angus bulls as a prominent local cattle farmer and deacon of a nearby Methodist Church. For the first time, Jesse realized that not all crooks were unshaven, unwashed and foul- talking like his father. Crooks also wear white shirts, ties and suits, drive clean big cars, and pray on Sundays from the first pew.

Two years after Sam disappeared, Mary died an early death from cigarettes, poor diet, and the anguish of being married to Sam. Two brothers, Henry and Harry, lied about their ages and joined the Army to get away from the poverty. Jesse never heard from them, which hurt, as he and Henry were very close. Harry was too mean and dumb to cause anyone to become close to him or even like him.

As boys, young Henry and Jesse ran endlessly through the Loess Hills of western Iowa. This long chain of small mountains ran for nearly two hundred miles along the entire western border of Iowa. They would play hunter, hide-and-seek, Indian fighter, and bandits. The lack of toys did not limit their imagination. A long stick became a gun, a sharp stick became a spear, and a large native fern leaf became a shield.

They loved the mysterious feeling of the area. The rounded top small mountains were cut by nature in various directions by deep valleys descending onto wide valley floors filled with short grasses. Quail, pheasants, deer and turkeys were bountiful.

During those days of youth, the Marvin boys often found relics of prehistoric animals buried years long ago when glaciers froze the sea and dropped deposits of extremely rich soil as the seas receded. They also found caves, with an occasional arrow head or spear point, where Indians hid from warring neighbors or the predatory white-man. These caves were their secret escape from a harsh life. They would often hover in them, telling tales of the ghosts of Indian warrior that roomed the land looking for revenge.

Despite the hardships, he liked where he lived and liked his life. After Mary died in the winter of 1999, he stayed with his Aunt Gladys and continued to go to school at Pisgah. He found that he enjoyed learning about facts that were new to his limited world. He grew up without money, a job, or guidance, but his life as a petty thief was evolving.

Pisgah was a dying town. Its populace was moving away for lack of work, and its businesses were closing. But some proud and stubborn people hung on and called it home. The limited number of people who might be witnesses and the under-manned law enforcement personnel allowed Jesse to engage in various forms of petty theft without legal risk. He was inherently smart, but a failure at school.

He could not see the relevance in any of the subjects and the need for homework. The one exception to his resistance to formal education was the function and use of a computer. His initial attraction to the computer world was based on betting and winning computer games. He was a master at letting the rich boys win a few games and increase the stakes. He seldom lost and always had enough money to satisfy his meager wants. A bottle of Pepsi and a hamburger on Saturday were the highlight of his week.

In his quest for improved computer knowledge, he befriended a young nerd, James Perlman. James was void of any social skills but was extremely well-versed regarding computers and video games. Every day after school, Jesse would go to James' home and they would sit silently at the computer. For James this relationship was as close as he could come to having a friend. For Jesse it was a forum for learning all he could about finding endless information on the developing web and winning at video games.

Jesse was short and thin. His light brown hair was always shaggy, he seldom shaved and his clothes were constantly rumpled. An iron and ironing-board were luxuries. He stunk from nonexistent bathing habits.

49

The rich boys were often deceived by his appearance and were quick to try to beat him at their latest video games. The only notable thing about him was his green reptilian eyes and, when he concentrated, a tendency to repeatedly lick his lips. Not surprisingly, he earned the name "The Lizard."

He was expelled from high school as a third year freshman in May of 1995 when he was caught stealing lunch room supplies by the Pisgah High School football coach. The big bullying coach roughed him up when he was caught red-handed. Later, the coach did not press legal charges when he found his dog and a stray cat decapitated and spread on his car hood accompanied by a note. "Looks like it rained cats and dogs last night, Coach."

Stealing and reselling school supplies to the students weren't his only early business ventures. No one ever connected him to the missing one hundred gallons of gas taken weekly from the fleet of school buses, the missing tools from shop or the missing computers from the business classes. Being expelled was costly. It deprived him of the chance to quietly snoop in the different rooms for marketable items. Expulsion, however, proved to be a fortuitous positive event.

CHAPTER NINE

"Education Is An Admirable Thing, But It Is Well To Remember From Time To Time That Nothing That Is Worth Knowing Can Be Taught."

OSCAR WILDE.

✶✶✶✶✶

Any successful business founder must initially identify the proper market niche. In this pursuit, mistakes can occur and initial market focus often shifts to more realistic markets. The successful foresighted leader is quick to admit initial failure and even quicker to identify alternative markets.

After his banishment from school, Jesse realized he was alone in the cold world. The easy market of cheating students and tricking gullible teachers was lost. His survival instincts, however, kicked into high gear and he began to search for new avenues to make money.

While he was contemplating alternatives, he broke into his friend James Perlman's home when the family was at an evening church meeting. He took James' TV, Play Station and all the related games. James' father's HP lap-top computer was a bonus score for this nocturnal venture. As he made his last trip from the Perlman house with the computer, he giggled. "Looks like I will not get invited back for a friendly games." he thought to himself.

Though various petty thefts, Jesse saved enough to buy a 1980 rusting Chevy pick-up. He spent the summer of 1995 wandering the small towns of the area looking for a new venture. One very humid July evenings, the answer became obvious.

EVERY FRIDAY was pay-day for the local workers. They usually ended their week at the only bar in Pisgah's: Frank's Uptown Beer Hall. Jesse noticed that as they drank away their meager earnings, they always would be visited in the unlit alleys by a tall, fat Hispanic. The large stranger's car plates were from Monona County. That meant they were from nearby Onawa, as it was the only town of any size with any Hispanic residents.

The pattern was always the same. After a little cheap liquor, the hill country boys' appetites quickly switched to smoking pot, not drinking cheap booze. Pouring cheap Hawkeye brand vodka, scotch and bourbon into long ago emptied Absolute, Johnnie Walker Red and Jack Daniels bottles was Frank's normal practice. The wacky-weed sales always occurred in an alley between the bar and the Old Home Filler-Up Cafe, Jesse's favorite eating place. The business at the bar consistently stopped about 10 p.m. as pot became the preference. A few minutes after the bar cleared, Frank would appear and chase the Hispanics away with a shot gun.

He saw his new market with crystal clear vision. His visit with Frank was short and blunt.

"If I can get a supply of pot, keep the Mexicans away, and you get 1/3 of the profits, would you welcome me in your place?"

"Son, if you can get that done, you are welcome in my place and my brother's places in Moorhead and Ute. But the Hispanics' seem to be the only local source of that wacky-weed. They are awful big for a little pecker-head like you."

He waited till the next payday and hung around the bar. When the Hispanics arrived, he went into the alleyway alone. A large, brown-skinned man with a growling voice motioned him closer.

"One ounce of Mexican Red for $25, you interested skinny white boy?"

Jesse nodded and held out the money as he walked into the shadows toward the monstrous image. The long braided hair and beard marred by scars were intimidating. Ramon Contreras watched, without concern, the approach of the small, shaggy, unshaven and rumpled man. The face with burning green eyes and flicking tongue was obscured by the old John Deere logoed hat pulled down, barely above his eyes.

Jesse moved forward without the least amount of fear or trepidation. As Ramon reached for the money, he felt a sharp pain on his throat.

"I have a razor sharp fish-skinning knife on your neck, big man. One move and you will be bleeding all over this alley. I don't want to hurt you. I want to do business. Sell me your pot for half price and I will triple what you sell in a week. In a month I will sell five times what you are currently doing. We all win. Blink if you agree!"

Ramon stared down motionlessly into the reptilian green eyes staring from under the hats bill. The swishing tongue was nearly hypnotizing. He knew he was likely dead in a few seconds.

While he was not mathematically gifted, Ramon understood the wisdom of the proposal and handed over his nightly inventory of ten ounces of pot. Jesse removed the knife from his throat and entered the bar.

"See you next week, Senor Ramon. Same time! Same place! Bring double the inventory."

Within a month, Jesse exceeded his promises and had expanded his business to three more towns, thanks to referrals from Frank and his happy brothers. Luckily, Frank never asked for an accounting. He was happy with his new-found $2000 dollars per month and free pot for his family and himself. Ramon was a hero to his boss, and the supply increased.

Jesse finally got the courage to try a little pot. He had watched the local boys inhale it and hold it in for what seemed like minutes. Then they would talk about how great they felt and how mellow they were becoming. Jesse was always scared of trying it for the same reason he never drank hard liquor. He feared being out of control. He had seen his dad do some crazy things when he was drunk.

But, he had to try what Ramon claimed was, "Great Mexican Shit."

On his first experiment, he inhaled and coughed violently as he tried to keep the smoke in his lungs. The pungent sweet smell was nice, but nothing special. He tried again and again with the same results. After a while, he threw the roach away and went home with a head-ache and aching lungs from coughing.

"Where does this mellow stuff and great feeling come from?" he thought as he opened a cold can of Millers. This stuff was for selling not using.

Within a year, he was making more money than he ever could spend. He felt like a rich person and bought a used 50x10 trailer house and a 40 acre parcel three miles west of Pisgah on a high hill overlooking the Missouri River bottom land. He never tired of looking at the sunset from this special location 800 feet above the crop-filled flat land below.

The location was perfectly situated for security and privacy. It was protected on the east by a heavy forest of ancient oaks. To the west was a steep cliff falling hundreds of feet to the valley below. The north side fell quickly to a long and wide valley covered with short grass. It was an ideal secret exit route. On the south was a long, gradual, low grass-covered slope running for a quarter mile up to his hilltop location. It was the only way to access the John Deere green colored trailer resting atop the ridge.

The trailer house sat high on the ridge overlooking the main road between Pisgah and Little Sioux. The road was extremely steep. It had been carved into the side of the huge hill long ago by talented contractors, used by stagecoaches, horseback mounted thieves and Model A owners for a century. Jesse had a perfect view of traffic coming toward him.

He loved to roam these hills when he wasn't selling pot and expanding his sales-force in other towns. As he wandered and listened to the chatter of squirrels, the cries of turkeys and pheasants, and the cawing of huge black crows, he was alone with unrestricted time to think.

He had heard all the legends. These quiet giants were created by an ocean, by a melting glacier, or they were the result of an ancient wind storm. He could not care less how these hills came to be. What he saw in them was opportunity. He was about to start his own plan for increased production and elimination of a middle-man level of costs.

CHAPTER TEN

"It's So Much Easier To Suggest Solutions When You Don't Know Too Much About The Problem."

M ALCOLM F ORBES

*****

As a business enters into its growth cycle, leadership must always evaluate how to cut cost and increase production in order to move profits to a higher level of success. Performing the same way every day will predestine a company to an early maturity and decline. Changing old methods and processes is the biggest early challenge faced by any emerging business; it requires self examination and adoption of new untried alternatives.

In his wanderings through his secret trails, Jesse noticed that volunteer marijuana plants were abundant on the east slope of hills which were not dramatically steep and were not filled with trees. He started to carry a large gray canvas bag and harvest these tall yellow-green jagged edged weeds in the fall.

The harvest was plentiful as the slopes were extremely fertile, which was the nature of loess soils. Each day after his walk, he carefully stripped the four-foot tall jagged leaf plants of their seeds and dried the leaves in the back half of his trailer-house. The only problems were the pungent smell from the drying leaves and the accompanying incidental insects, which made his new home nearly uninhabitable.

After a few years of trying to sleep, ward off insects, and ignoring the smell of the drying leaves, he recognized this production problem needed quick and decisive attention. Having his home as the drying and warehousing location for his business wouldn't cut it. He immediately initiated a plan for expanding his warehousing and increasing his production. For the past three years, his market was expanding and could easily absorb new volume. If he could rely on self-produced pot, it would allow the gradual elimination of buying from Ramon. He had just learned the meaning of increased margins.

The north side of the hill, where Jesse's trailer-house majestically sat, was steeply sloped to a flat valley floor that ran gradually for miles. The valley floor was extensive; it was a mile wide. This valley provided a perfectly concealed approach to his home. It would be a significant part of his new warehouse/production facility solution.

The three Sharpe brothers were local contractors. They were all connoisseurs of Jesse's pot and were always broke. They were unreliable and rarely got to work before the day was half completed. Their bad habits, front-end loader and excavator equipment, and dirt moving skills were perfect for Jesse's plan.

All three Sharpe brothers were 50 pounds overweight, wore shoulder length shaggy brown greasy hair, and five day old stubble beard. They were pleasant guys who were always laughing and telling and retelling jokes and rumors. Their bib overalls were washed once a week no matter how dirty they became. Their denim shirts proudly displayed multi-colored patches over numerous holes. Each of their aging pickups was coated with several stickers proudly declaring the latest redneck quotes.

"I will give you each a 100 dollars a day and all the pot you can smoke if you would dig a cave under the hill where my trailer stands."

The Sharpe boys each nodded in unison, like bobble-head dolls. Jesse laid out a rough drawing of how they could make his cave facility. It would be over 150 feet long by 90 feet wide with a 20 foot high ceiling. The hilltop bearing the trailer would be four feet thick and supported by reinforcing steel girders. The entire facility would be invisible. The tree covered valley located to the north end would easily camouflage transportation routes to and from the cave.

The Sharpe brothers were ecstatic about steady pay and pot. In their rare sober moments, they improved on Jesse's sketchy drawings. They determined exactly how to create air-circulation, how to hide a heating and air-conditioning unit, and how to cover the north side entrance with trees and bushes to escape detection. But, they pointed out, they were broke and would need lumber, heating and air-conditioning equipment, garage doors and drywall.

Jesse promised a quick solution to the material needs. They provided him with lists of items and started excavation with gusto waiting for the promised material. They actually arrived early the first day: nine-thirty.

Jesse eagerly jumped into his rusting black 1980 Chevrolet pickup. With lumber dimensions and quantity requirements in hand, he commenced to visit the lumberyards in the area. The small dying lumber operations did not provide a solution, but their complaining about the large store competition provided the answer.

He easily solved the source of wood issue when he found out when and how the truckers delivered full loads to the Sioux City Lowe's Store. The truckers always arrived early to the Lowes' sites and slept in their trucks waiting for the stores to open which allowed them to start the unloading process.

Early one morning, Terry Jones, an overweight driver of 30, sat in the large sleeper cab of his Kenworth truck cab. He was bored, nibbling on his third jelly filled donut while resting in the back parking area of the Sioux City Lowe's store. He looked, with no concern, at the approaching scruffy little man. He was wearing a Lowe's logoed hat and coat and holding up a fresh cup of coffee. As Jones reached out of his cab window for the coffee, he never noticed the fish skinning knife till it was directly on his throat.

"Wanna make a quick $1000 or die, tubby boy?"

The decision was easy. Terry Jones slid over out of the driver's seat and put the blindfold on as directed. He was released from the truck five miles from Moville, Iowa, thirty miles east of Sioux City.

"Here are your five new 100 dollar bills. I have your name and address. Five hundred more will show up next week if you ain't stupid and follow my directions. I want ya to take your time, walk to town. After a good meal, call your company and tell them how this big red-headed, eye-patched wearing, crook kidnapped ya and threw you out as he headed south to Des Moines. Is that too hard to remember fat boy?"

Jones swallowed deep and nodded.

"By the way, fat boy, if ya screw me, I have your address, and your wife and two boys' pictures. Be too bad if somebody would hurt them."

Jesse headed the truck and trailer south to Pisgah using only dirt and narrow farm to market roads. The Sharpes' equipment made it easy to unload the cache of lumber products. A quick five mile drive to the Missouri River provided a wet and final 40 foot deep resting place for the truck and semi-trailer. His only regret was the five mile walk back to his trailer. He arrived before the Sharpes' normal arrival time, at the crack of noon.

Jesse found this process too easy. He decided to repeat another snatch before anyone figured out there was a pattern. The next morning, he arrived and selected a truck full of drywall panels. He repeated the process. This time he brought along a small motorcycle to avoid the five mile walk from the Missouri River which consumed another truck and semi-trailer at a different, but equally deep, location.

The following morning he visited a Home Depot in Council Bluffs and found a load of overhead garage doors and automatic opener units on a truck waiting to be unloaded.

A few days later he stumbled on a new office building in the Old Town section of Omaha. That night he returned and stole the trailer bearing three uncrated heating and air-conditioning units.

He was finding the early morning rides from the Missouri River dumping sites on his stolen yellow Honda motorcycle quite exhilarating. Watching the river quietly swallow $200,000 vehicles was also fascinating.

The Sharpe boys were ecstatic at having so much building material to utilize in this venture, but their pace was unchanged. This euphoria ended one fall evening when Jesse called them into his trailer house. He had cold beer and pot laid out on his rickety wood table. His green eyes focused on each of them, one at a time. His tongue flicked about wetting his lips.

"Boys, enjoy the night. From now on you is at work by seven, you quit at dark, and you get this project done by August which is two months away."

He glared at them, his tongue flicking and his green eyes piercing as he cleaned his finger nails with his ancient fishing knife.

"Incidentally, the size of the project has doubled. I want the warehouse walled off east of the entry area. My office and living area will be in the part west of the entry. I have found some nice wood flooring material and coated drywall for it. I also have a couple of new plasma TVs for you to mount after you put up my new satellite dish. All that great fertile dirt from the cave will be spread on that valley behind my hill so I can put my new crop in this spring."

The three double chins gulped in unison as they realized it was not business as usual. Sweat started to bead on their stubble covered jowls.

"Here are the new drawings. If you don't get this done right and on time, you're dead. Oh, by the way, if you breathe a word about this material, you all go to jail for theft and murder of those drivers that hauled all that material you will install. Drink-up and have fun now, unless you have questions, **IF I WAS NOT CLEAR!**

The message was clear. The impact was chilling. They would never know that none of the drivers had died, and each one had profited from losing their load to The Lizard.

The Sharpe boys realized this was not a threat to be taken lightly and performed beyond their normal pace and skills. They finished on time. The hill looked to a passing observer to be unchanged. However, under the hill's cap laid a warehouse with air circulation to allow quick drying, a small grinding operation, a seed-separating operation and Jesse's pad.

None of the manufacturing processes were state of the art, but they worked. Jesse was ready to receive his first crop of pot which he had hand-planted in early May.

The relationship with Ramon continued to grow through the summer. Ramon was delighted to keep delivering more products. It eliminated long nights of work and risk. He didn't even notice in the late fall around harvest time that the amount of orders started to dwindle. At this same time, Jesse started a non-stop process of complaining about the market drying up and the risk getting higher.

By 2002, Jesse's pot crop production was expanding. He had never been so rich. Ramon finally noticed that Jesse was starting to miss meetings. He knew he needed to solve the problem before his boss came down on him. One fall day he found Jesse eating a lunch of breaded deep fried tenderloin and greasy French fries, the noon special at his favorite cafe in Pisgah.

"We need to talk, little white boy."

"Look, Ramon, I is tired of the risk. I is tired of working nights. And this market ain't what it was. The farm prices are terrible. These farmers get less than two dollars a bushel for corn and four dollars for soybeans. They are just hanging on. The big, dumb farm boys are broke. The jobs for the local boys are drying up. The fellers are moving away. These little towns is dying. This ain't worth the risk. The bar owners have chased me off dozens of times and threatened to call the cops if I come back. I may do a few more deliveries, but I am done."

Ramon had no answer to this obvious problem. The little dirty white boy talked like he was retarded. He was believable. The market was likely dying, just like all the towns in this area. Ramon checked on Jesse's story and tried a few times to sell at his usual taverns. Just as Jesse said, the owners chased him off with a shotgun or a huge bouncer. One even had the County Sheriff follow him to the county boundary line. He reported to his boss that the market was dying. They needed to move on or find a new product.

Jesse's plan worked perfectly. The bar owners all loved the ploy and quickly agreed to a new delivery location in their storage room, not their alleys. He now dominated the market without spilling a drop of blood.

CHAPTER ELEVEN

"You Can Get Much Further With A Kind Word And A Gun Than You Can With A Kind Word Alone."

A L   C A P O N E

*****

As a business grows in volume and success, the need to protect its assets from the intrusions of competitors becomes imperative. Start-up companies are rarely noticed, but as success occurs the previously complacent competitor will examine every alternative to derail emergent company's progress. Security of key assets must be an early priority.

Jesse knew with his expanded production capacity, he needed to find new locations with more local pot-heads willing to pay for the low-grade product. His pot would not be sought by the elite consumer, but his Loess Hill's Gold was popular in the small Iowa towns for one obvious reason, it was cheap. Before he embarked on expanding his market, he needed to make sure to protect his current operation. It was netting him $20,000 a week after paying off his local distributors and local law enforcement.

His competition was temporarily gone, but they were still occasionally around checking their lost pot market. They were content to push a new drug called crystal-meth. He knew if they saw him as real competition, they would try to eliminate him. If he tried to eliminate his competition by muscle tactics, he would find more violence than he wanted or was able to deal with.

So rather than have a head-on turf war, he decided he would simply keep convincing his Mexican suppliers that small town Iowa was a dying market. His meeting with Ramon had gone a long way in achieving that goal. Several follow-up meetings had Ramon convinced. Jesse's solution was easy. He would simply undercut their price for meth and watch their customers go away. He saw Wal-Mart do the same thing to small town business and figured it must be a good idea.

HIS METHODS WORKED. By 2004, the Mexican sales forces had abandoned the area. Just in case his competition got wise to his poor-boy methods and tried to muscle him, He decided to recruit his own team of security guards. He was small, and while he had a mean streak and no morals about life or limb, he knew he was no match for big thugs like Ramon.

He drove around the small towns of southwest Iowa and found big guys, but they were too fat and lazy from donuts and pizza at the local C-stores. He also found mean men, but they were void of trained skills. He gave up on local talent.

Web-surfing crimes in the area, he discovered there were a large number of transplanted Bosnians in the Omaha area. He read about their civil war and knew he had found an answer. He ran an ad for unlicensed security guards in the Omaha World Herald and received 50 applicants. Each night for a week, he hopped in his pickup and head to Omaha to interview the final ten.

He picked a thin dark-skinned man named Rufkin because of the multiple scars on his shaved head and large calloused hands. Rufkin's display of knife-throwing sealed his selection. He took a beer can out of a patrons hand from 20 feet and attached it to the adjacent wall with an eight-inch stiletto. Otto was selected next because of his brute size and strength. He was a mastodon of a man; six-foot eight inches, 300 pounds, and extremely defined muscles displayed by a nearly skin tight shirt. Pumping iron was his hobby. His close cropped black hair, unblinking cold black eyes, and beak like nose were intimidating.

Both men were hired with one goal, follow him and keep him safe. They were well-paid, ignored offers of pot and reported to work on time. Jesse found their work ethics different from the Harrison county populace. Within two months he doubled their salaries.

AFTER A YEAR of working with his newly hired bodyguards, Jesse discovered that they were very fluent in English and well educated. He quickly recognized that they had extremely well honed survival instincts. They were survivors of hell. They trusted no one. Rufkin reviewed the terrain and suggested that the grass filled south-slope gradually ascending to his trailer-house was in need of better protection. It was too open and could be easily approached or watched.

He was delighted with the solution. Rufkin came up with the concept of placing rotating cameras with night vision in the trailer with monitors in the cave warehouse under the trailer. The entire slope and approaching area would be constantly under surveillance.

Rufkin also added the idea of placing hidden cameras a mile in each direction of the road leading to the cave warehouse. They would provide early detection of approaching intruders. Otto installed cameras suspended in trees to provide day and night observation of the northern approach which ran through a long, wandering valley.

As a further defensive measure, the trailer was loaded with dynamite in case the intruders needed to be eliminated. The trailer's windows were lined with a series of M-16 automatic rifles on tripods that were controlled by joy sticks in Jesse's office beside the monitors.

The cameras, monitors, installation and training, were all compliments of Bartine Melovic, a Bosnian friend of Rufkin. Bartine had converted his electrical engineer degree and the knack for survival into a profitable and deadly business in his home town of Kosovo. Jesse paid him double the price.

Jesse loved his new security systems and guards. He also realized that his ever increasing production and delivery system needed even further enhancements to avoid detection. The Sharpe brothers relocated several large local trees in front of the north entrance and created a visual barrier hiding the 20 foot high retractable warehouse door which was painted dirt brown to blend in with the hillside. The north entrance road winding through the adjacent valley looked like any farm access road, except it was lined with cameras located in trees disguised as bird houses. They provided a 24/7 picture of all users.

RUFKIN'S SISTER STELLA was hired to monitor the cameras on the roads and the southern approach to the trailer-house. For an additional fee, Rufkin threw in sexual access to Stella whenever Jesse was so inclined. Jesse doubted she knew about this term.

She was approximately 30 years old, small, thin, athletic, with black curly shoulder length hair, and olive skin. She had a small featured attractive face with brown sad eyes, a thin turned up nose and a nice, but infrequently displayed, thin-lipped smile. She was very polite to him.

Although she was not beautiful, she was better looking than anyone he had ever degraded in the past. He felt he had negotiated a great bargain. He was unsure how to approach her on the sex issue so he avoided it. But he often spent unnecessary time with her asking to be trained on the security system. She was starting to warm to his inquisitive nature and talked extensively to him about the equipment and systems. He knew she was far better educated than him and was intimidated. He was still not sure how to bring up his sex for hire deal.

STELLA BOBAN was a survivor. She had grown up in the outskirts of Sarajevo. Her family were all college educated. Her father was an accountant who raised a family on the rich hills west of the very modern city which had once welcomed the world at a Winter Olympics. His income was adequate but was supplemented by raising crops in his vast garden. The breakup of Yugoslavia was at first welcomed as the oppression of the tyrannical Tito was ended. The craziness that followed was unexpected.

The war in Bosnia and Herzegovina involved the Bosnian Serbs and Croats and the Herzog-Bosnian, led and supplied by Serbia. When the Bosnian Serb forces attacked the Republic of Bosnia and Herzegovina to secure more territory, Her world turned upside down. Her mother and father simply disappeared in the ethnic cleansing of the Serb forces. She and her brother Rufkin hid in the hills in an old hunting cabin on their small farm. Rufkin worked with local resistant fighters and regularly brought her food from his latest victim. His repeated cuts showed he worked up close in his efforts to rid the area of the crazy killing process. He survived the siege of Sarajevo with the help of his new friend, a giant named Otto Tudman.

When NATO finally intervened and brought an end to the conflict with the Dayton Agreement, Stella was ready to move on. She had survived two rapes and had learned how to use sex to control men. She had also learned that she possessed a high IQ and was a constant reader of multiple self help books. She was intrigued with the computer and internet world.

She and Rufkin made connections with her mother's brother in Omaha through the Red Cross. By spending the money Rufkin and Otto had accumulated by stealing from their dead war victims the necessary paper work was secured to immigrate.

Uncle Enver was kind, but poor. He took them into his three bedroom home on the rundown north side of Omaha. Stella, like all of the poor Bosnians, was ambitious. She started to work in multiple jobs: a cook at McDonalds, a warehouse person at Best Buy, and a clerk at Home Depot.

She worked hard and discovered she had a unique talent for learning the English language. She was promoted to a full-time clerk at the local Best Buy where she spent off the clock hours working with the Geek Squad and expanding her knowledge of computers and the internet. Flirting with and occasionally making out with one of the Geeks accelerated the learning process.

Rufkin was slower at learning the new language, but soon fell into a small tight- knit group of Bosnian thieves and enforcers. The remaining Mafia operations in the Omaha area found it better to outsource enforcement than to develop their own muscle. Otto developed a full-time schedule as a local bouncer at several upbeat bars. His ominous size also attracted him as a bodyguard for hire. The "bodyguard for hire" ad of Jesse's changed their lives.

JESSE KNEW HIS PRODUCTION was a major key to his operation. He had to hide the ten acres of pot growing in the valley north of the cave warehouse. The answer became obvious as Jesse drove to

Pisgah for his usual breaded deep fried tenderloin sandwich and greasy fries at the Old Home Filler-up Cafe. He had just finished a busy morning delivering a week's inventory of pot to his 10 salesmen and was enjoying his meal.

He loved this run-down old cafe. It had been the focal point of a series of TV ads in the early 1980s for Omaha baked "Old Home Bread." He loved the ads when C.W. McCall drove to town to see his girlfriend Mavis at the cafe and had coffee and apple pie while she flirted with him. The series of convoy songs, ads, and a Kris Kristofferson movie titled "Convoy," all came from that meager series of ads. Chip Davis, the advertising man who came up with the truck convoy idea, made a bundle and reverted to his love of music with a new group, Mannheim Steamroller.

As he slowly drove away from lunch, the solution occurred to him as he watched the farmers planting corn. By late July the corn would be six to seven feet tall, a perfect perimeter barricade around his field of pot. That night he solved the matter by stealing a tractor, with an attached planter filled with robust Pioneer corn seed.

The next morning, since he did not know how to operate a planter, he had a Sharpe brother plant 12 rows of corn around the entire pot field. In a few months the valuable pot-crop in the center would be obscured.

After the planting was completed, he was happy and proud of his accomplishments. He took a shower, shaved, put on clean jeans and a clear denim work shirt. He grabbed a cold six pack of Miller beer and a bag of potato chips and went to the monitoring area in the cave. He knew Stella was working. They ate and drank, and she continued to educate him on how the system worked.

He wanted desperately to talk about and have sex, but he was afraid. His horrible upbringing had provided him little knowledge about women or sex. His mother had told him nothing. His dad always changed the subject and referred him to his mother. His friends while they talked big were all very ignorant on the subject. His few brief encounters with the two local homemaker-whores in Woodbine had been embarrassing. They were so ugly, and he was too quick. Twenty dollars for 30 seconds of fumbling sex seemed unfair, even for sex.

CHAPTER TWELVE

" In The Broth, Creativity Varies Inversely With The Number Of Cooks Involved."

BERNICE FITZGIBBONS

*****

As a company emerges beyond the start-up stage, it must determine if its current market will allow growth to new and more successful levels. If the current market is limited in its potential, new markets, which can be achieved by way of the leverage from the current market, must be identified and engaged with enthusiasm.

After three years, Jesse had built a significant market through his own efforts. He knew it was time to expand through the use of other people's skills. He had created a network based on three local friends that had contracted with him as sales representatives for 60 towns in small rural western Iowa and eastern Nebraska. Instinctively, Jesse had developed his own version of Avon's pyramid marketing system. No pink cars were involved.

Each territorial manager purchased his area's quota of product, repackaged it, re-priced it and delivered it to his next multilevel of distribution. No one beyond his three territorial managers knew of him or the source. Since each of them feared his Lizard reputation, He felt secure.

He had an inherent distrust of everyone. It was not surprising that he decided to run his own version of quality control, price control, and marketing techniques. Every few days when there was a lull in the growing season, Jesse took off in his increasingly rusting 1980 Chevy pick-up. He would quietly drive into a town, locate a local store and buy a hat or coat bearing a logo from a local business or sports team. After a couple of beers in the town's most active bar, he was quickly provided with directions as to who to see for a little bag of Mary-Jane.

Then pulling the new cap down so his piercing green eyes were not visible, he'd made a buy. He'd in a soft voice, bargain with the salesman, trying to verify if he was aware of who was the local law. But in the end he always bought and left quietly. After such visits, more than one young salesman got his own territory. A few got their fingers dislocated by Otto for over pricing or cutting the quantity. A couple just disappeared.

Rumors spread among the sales system about The Lizard's visits and how he hated cheaters or potential snitches. The only common denominator was that no one remembered what he looked like.

AT THE END OF THE GROWING SEASON of 2009, Jesse intuitively recognized he needed more production, more salesmen and, more importantly, a trusted sales manager. He asked Stella if it was possible through the internet to do national searches to locate people. After one day's work, she quickly arranged for Harrison Warehousing, Inc with its new fake Federal Tax ID Number to engage four Internet search companies. Each entity proudly acclaimed their ability to locate anyone. Three were shams. But one was for real. Within a week, his brother, Henry Alfred Marvin, was located in a rundown portion of Phoenix. Henry was flown to Omaha for a reunion with Jesse.

They drove to a 70 year old pink block building in nearby Crescent, Iowa for a lengthy and filling dinner at the Pink Poodle Restaurant. At first the conversation was slow and strained. They found it difficult to ignore their painful childhood. They mostly talked about how they were enjoying the endless supply of home-made bread, mashed potatoes, beef gravy, and an enormous slice of aged beef rib roast.

Eventually, the brotherly spirit started to emerge. They talked non-stop on the drive back to Pisgah about the business Jesse had created. They frequently digressed to retell their recollections of the exploring and games they enjoyed as boys roaming the Loess Hills. By the time they arrived at Jesse's cave home, Henry had a clear picture of his opportunity of being named Head of Sales.

Life had been cruel before Henry ran away. As the oldest brother, he often stood up for his mother and suffered when father Sam was drunk and mean. Six years in the army had not been great, as he got stuck in a truck that delivered supplies throughout Iraq and Afghanistan. An occasional bomb, bullet, or ambush had left his nerves in a shattered state. Sam's alcohol gene took control and the army gave Henry an honorable discharge or jail choice after a fight with his new bride. The marriage ended quickly, luckily with no children.

After his second stay in jail for drunken and disorderly conduct, Henry got lucky. He found a fellow veteran who took him in a hammerlock wrestling hold to repeated AA meetings. Surprisingly, Henry listened and took control of his behavior. He had been sober three years and was driving a truck for a local delivery company.

Jesse's advance of rent for six months, a promise of a good salary and use of a rusty but well maintained Ford 150 pickup sealed the deal. Henry proved to be energetic and in 90 days added two more territorial managers that covered 12 more towns in rural Iowa. No pot-heads needs went unanswered in the western half of Iowa.

THE PROBLEM of having enough products for the increasing capacity of the sales force was Jesse's next challenge. He plugged in his Johnny Cash CDs, grabbed a cool six-pack of Millers and cruised the winding, roughly maintained back roads of the Loess Hills in Harrison and Monona counties.

He was initially looking for land to buy and convert to his production needs. Each time he stopped to talk to a farmer, his interest in buying their farm was promptly rejected. He was amazed as the farmers were weathered, thin, and wearing tattered clothes. Their farm values had recently shot up with the increase global demand for corn and soybeans. However, they were often mired in debt accumulated during the thin years and by buying too much new equipment in the recently developing good years. These proud people simply would not part with their land even if they were one step from foreclosure. Poor but proud people were hard to deal with. Jesse couldn't figure out if they were poor because they were too proud, or if they were just blindly stubborn.

The solution to the product supply issue was to locate hill-land farmers, who were typically the most financially challenged, and hire them to grow marijuana plants on one of their most obscured plots of rich hill land. The selected land must be hidden from view and be surrounded by tall corn to avoid observation. The arrangement was simple; the farmer kept the corn and received triple the local cash rent price for their pot producing land. They would fertilize the new crop twice a year with fertilizer delivered to them at night, compliments of Jesse's midnight visit to local grain co-op's storage sheds.

The farmers would not take part in the pot harvest as a team of pickers with wagons and cutters would, without prior notice, simply appear, collect the product and disappear. The farmers were warned by him, with all the fear that his reptilian green eyes and flicking tongue could convey, that no one could know of this arrangement, as they were the only grower in the area with this special deal. He always made it clear that if anyone found out about their special deal a picture of their special field would be sent to the Feds. Within two months in early 2009, Jesse had arranged 10 of these special, and supposedly exclusive, growing arrangements. The early down-payment of half the rent always sealed the deal.

He was extremely proud of the results of his tireless work. He desperately needed to brag to someone about these recent accomplishments. With a six-pack of Miller, two bags of chips, and a blanket in hand, he asked Stella to watch the sunset with him at his special place. They walked up the highest hill in the area located about a half mile from his trailer. He gallantly spread the blanket on a flat ridge-top, popped a couple of beers, and ripped open the chips.

Below them were endless acres of wildflowers and prairie grasses covering the slope; yellow, white, and pink colors intertwined. As they held hands and looked west, the 50 mile wide Missouri River Valley presented a panoramic abstract mural of varied shades of green and gold. The lights of the small towns were commencing to blink. The sun was a burning orange color as it slowly disappeared over the Nebraska hill line to the west. The night birds were darting about; swallows sweeping up bugs, golden finches gorging themselves on prairie-grass seeds, and pheasants crying for a mate.

He was at peace and had a chance to brag. He had a sales force that covered all of Iowa and most of Nebraska. He had a fleet of over 100 delivery vehicles. He had 300 acres of Iowa pot under production in obscure fields throughout the Loess Hills. His competition was gone without a fight. His cave warehouse and production facility was working flawlessly and appeared to be just another doomed shaped hill.

He was not sure Stella understood his babbling. His English was not as good as hers. They were on an equal footing as she was trying to learn the new language, and he had never tried to learn it.

They discussed the weather, the beauty of the evening and what Jesse had accomplished. He tried to ask about her and her family, but there was no response. Without a word, she downed her second beer, disrobed and gave him a full year course in sex education in three hours. Jesse as usual was a quick learner. They spent the night under the stars, and he awoke with a grin still frozen on his face. Jesse found himself gently holding her and experienced an epiphany had by few men; being gentle, interested and patient can be seductive.

BY 2011, THE FARM ECONOMY had finally had a turn for the better as prices were up. However, many of the local farmers were still struggling with debts accumulated over many years and new high costs of production. Corporations had assembled large acreages. Small towns were decaying. Residents who had enough talent or ambition to acquire and hold a job either moved away or spent their lives on long commutes. The remaining population led a dreary life of trying to make a living from their small fields, watching their gardens become consumed by endless weeds, and talking about how the Republicans were to blame. All clearly recalled how good the good old days were. What the world needed was another F.D.R. Obama was not the savior he had promised to be.

Jesse prospered. His cash intake was up to six figures a week. His brother had found the AA life allowed his brain to recover and imagination to flourish. The Big Book and the initial 12 steps had succeeded in changing his life.

They were a dynamic duo. Jesse loved the camaraderie of having his brother near him. They joked like little boys, but planned like heartless crooks. Henry, like Jesse, had endless energy and love for excitement and money.

Henry frequented run-down bar after bar in the western half of Iowa, with incredible success. Despite the temptation, his commitment to AA allowed him to avoid having even one drink. He knew to an alcoholic one drink is too many and after that a thousand is not enough. He found it easy to find local bar owners who would look the other way and devote their back room to a pot sales office. It was also easy to find young men who at once had a high IQ, but were now trapped forever in a small town, addicted to pot, becoming lazy, and looking for easy money.

On a hot and sunny March morning, Stella called Jesse on his cell phone. "Quick, get up to the monitoring center. You need to see this. A fleet of three black GMC's are headed up the steep hill leading to Pisgah and will pass directly by your trailer-house."

Quickly, Rufkin and Otto were summoned to Jesse's office in his cave. Stella checked the remote operated guns in the trailer.

"This is where you earn your bonus by keeping my ass safe," Jesse yelled at the two bodyguards as they ran to their pre-assigned locations.

As the three GMC's stopped, six huge Hispanic men emerged and looked up the hill. Three of the big men started briskly walking up the hill. Jesse, with a six-pack of Miller in hand, emerged from the trailer and walked half way down the grassy slope. He stopped at the large blackberry bush cluster midway down the slope, which was the exact point where all the remote guns were aimed.

The three Hispanics were moving steadily up the dusty hill. They were all in black pants, white shirts, and each carried a Glock in a chest holster. They were well muscled, clean-cut and sweating profusely.

"My name is Pablo, or Paul to you, scruffy little white boy. These two are my friends, Juan and Marco. Our boss would like to meet you. Will you pay him the respect of coming to his air-conditioned car?"

Jesse popped a beer top and took a deep swallow.

"Have a cool beer guys? This weather is hot. Tell yer boss, I ain't fucking nuts. I am a little dumb white boy who used to sell a little pot for him. I ain't looking for a visit in his car."

Pablo was dumb-struck. "My boss will be very offended and will likely tell me to break your arm and drag you to this meeting."

Jesse's green eyes narrowed, his tongue switched from side to side. "Walk slowly down that hill, pig-fucker, and leave these two sweaty muscle-bound idiots here. Tell your boss there is a sharp-shooter trained on his car and these two boys is dead if I nod my head. If either the car moves or you try to shoot, you're all dead. I will meet him right where I stand, and we can talk about anything."

Pablo grinned and his evil brown eyes narrowed. "I doubt this bullshit, but I will talk to him. He will be angry."

Jesse took another deep pull on his beer and looked up into Pablo's sweating face. With an unblinking stare from his green eyes, his tongue swished from side to side.

"Tell him to come on up for a neighborly cold beer. Before he gets out of the car, have him call me on my cell at 712-555-0011, if he wants to talk."

Pablo walked slowly to the middle GMC and talked into a middle window after it was partially lowered. Jesse's phone rang. A heavily accented voice softly growled.

"You are an ignorant, arrogant little shit and you are bluffing."

" I may be ignorant, but I am not bluffing. These hillbilly boys is great hunters and shooters. One has a bead on your head right now. If that window even starts to move up, you are dead. I never bluff."

Instantly Jesse raised his beer in a salute. Juan's head exploded from a direct hit from a hollow-point 30-06 bullet. He fell in a heap at Jesse's feet.

The sound of the shot, echoed up the endless canyons, the birds stopped chirping and the world became silent. Juan's body lay still while it expelled his blood into the light brown soil. Two minutes passed. Jesse's cell rang.

"I will come up to speak to you."

Jesse took another pull on the beer and waved as he whispered into the cell-phone. "Welcome, amigo. Walk up the hill and meet me. We can talk about anything ya want."

The small Hispanic man, shaking his head emerged in slow motion from the middle GMC. He was dressed totally in black. His long-sleeve silk shirt and tailored pants were worth more than Jesse's trailer house.

He had a rough and pitted face with a nose that had been on the receiving end of more than one punch. His black hair was shiny, his eyes were masked by expensive mirrored sunglasses, and his heavily gold-chain clad skin was deep brown. As he scuffled slowly up the grass covered slope, the dry dust from the soil kicked-up to stain his black trousers to knee level. His frown intensified. He looked straight into Jesse's eyes for a long period.

"You may be a dirty, scrawny little hillbilly, but you aren't dumb and you aren't a small time dealer, amigo. Call me Rafaela."

Jesse gazed endlessly, as if he could see through the mirrored glasses.

"What can a little guy like me do for a rich gentlemen like you, amigo? Want a cool brew?"

"I am not sure we can do anything for you, Senor Jesse, except let you live."

"Mr. Rafaela, that sure is big of you. You don't understand. These Loess Hills and these small towns are my protection. I knew you were coming from the time you got off I-29 at River Sioux. The people around here love a guy called The Lizard."

Jesse took another deep pull on the beer. His tongue flicked with excitement.

"These special friends of The Lizard all have free cell phones and a couple of special warning numbers. They are very loyal. They get fresh steaks, pork-chops and a little beer money, and pot if they want, every month. They are always spreading rumors that this Lizard guy is everywhere. The locals, even the ministers, all love The Lizard as every town project gets donations in cash, wrapped up fancy in a band with a lizard logo on it."

"Amigo Jesse, we will talk again. Maybe we can learn how to work together. But, do not try to convince me you are a small time dealer or this market has dried-up. You fooled my idiot nephew Ramon, but I know a professional when I see one."

"Mucho gracias for the compliment. No one ever called me a professional at anything, except being a screw-up. Call this same number when you want to talk. By the way that was a good idea to not stay in that car." Jesse pumped his fist three times.

From atop the bluff overlooking the three black SUVs, Rufkin released the small shoulder launched missile. The middle car imploded in a pile of molten metal.

Intimidation of a competitor is essential in starting any negotiations!

CHAPTER THIRTEEN

"Any Organization Is Like A Septic Tank. The Really Big Chunks Rise To The Top."

JOHN IMHOFF

*****

As a business grows and prospers, it always becomes a target for acquisition by a larger competitor. Once that opportunity arises, the target company must move ahead very carefully as the merger process consumes endless amounts of time and energy and is frequently filled with half-truths, seducing, and confusion. Once a company starts the merger process, it is often hard to get off the back of the tiger without being devoured.

After a week, Jesse's phone finally rang. He had been nervous and not sure he wanted to start this process. A very crisp strong voice came through the microphone.

"This is Kurt Garcia in Cabo San Lucas, Mexico. My U.S. manager, Rafaela, says we need to talk. You have something I need. Your pot operation, crooked farmers, hidden warehouse, and security system are well done, but they are small time. Pot is too cheap and too available. It's not strong enough for the druggies that are our customers. I need your marketing, transportation, and warehouse system. Meet me and we will talk. Your safety is guaranteed, anyway you desire. You are missing a far bigger profit in not being in the business of meth."

"I need to think for a while. Life is good in these hills. I have all the beer I can drink, a couple of big TVs, and a sex-pot girlfriend. What more can a hill boy like me want?"

The phone was silent.

"Call if you want to talk, Senor Lizard."

JESSE THOUGHT ABOUT A WEEK before he replied. He called the cell number. A soft female voice answered.

"Jesse Marvin, wait a second for Mr. Garcia."

During the minute-long pause, he nearly hung-up. He was richer than he ever believed, he had steady sex, and he was safe. On their frequent trips to his special spot on the highest hill, Stella had tried repeatedly to talk him out of the idea of talking further with Garcia. Why risk it? Over the past few years they had accumulated a fortune. Their business ran on its own. The answer was easy. Jesse was greedy and loved the thrill.

"This is Kurt Garcia. When and where can we meet and get to know each other? Spring in Mexico is beautiful."

The call was short. Jesse quietly announced, "The first meeting would be a get-to-know each other session. I only work with people I like and trust. The location will be beside the huge Bass Pro display at the Omaha Sportsmen show next Wednesday."

Jesse paused. "Kurt, you will be surrounded by hundreds of hunters and sportsmen who all look alike. Some will be my men. Don't try any fast moves. Bring all the guns you want, but don't try to trick this little hillbilly."

"As we get to know each other, let's talk about how these negotiations go forward, Garcia. What's in it for you? What do you really want from this little Iowa boy, and how do I stay alive while we talk?"

"Senior Jesse, we will meet Wednesday."

Meanwhile, Stella had been on the Internet. Jesse wanted to know more about meth.

"This stuff is frightening, Jesse. Its real name is methamphetamine. It hooks people very quickly because it has the stimulus effect of increasing alertness, energy, and creates a rush of euphoria."

He looked long at Stella. "What is euphoria?

She smiled and touched his hand. "It's a quick feeling of being delighted and feeling wonderful all over your body. It's like when we have sex and you climax, only magnify it 10 times for hours of duration."

He smiled and patted her small but well shaped bottom. "Boy, how do I get this stuff?"

She winked at him. She faked a shy smile.

"Quiet and listen to me. I have done a lot of work on researching this subject. This shit is awful. It is highly addictive. Some experts say even one hit is enough to hook you. It can be smoked, injected, or swallowed. It causes your brain to release hormones called endorphins which causes euphoria. However, increased use causes part of the brain to be damaged and unable to properly produce endorphins. Then the dumb user thinks they aren't getting the right level of meth so they take more. This causes the brain to deteriorate even faster. Loss of memory, delusions, and paranoia is normal. Meth also causes 'meth-mouth' where the teeth blacken and decay. It also produces serious health issues from unsterilized needles, burns from melting the crystals, and lack of hygiene concern. All this leads to early death."

She continued to read from her printouts of her Internet work.

"You will like this. Sexual compulsion can be increased as the sex drive is accelerated, but a climax becomes harder to achieve. It can be taken as a powder, a smoke, or even a suppository."

"My butt aches just thinking like that. But, tell me more about this all-day sex and endless boner." She gave him a gentle shoulder punch and kiss on the cheek.

"Jesse, are you sure you want into this stuff? It looks like it's cheap to make. We have most of its components around here. We can get the anhydrous ammonia by stealing from the farmers fertilizer tanks and stealing or buying the over-the-counter cold medicine. With some help, we could make it in our cave and deliver it through our teams. But this stuff is bad. It kills people. Pot just makes them dumb and lazy."

He reached for two beers and grabbed her hand.

"Thanks for the hard work. A dummy like me could never have found all of this. I know you're scared. I am kind of buzzed-up for this new game, but I hear ya on the side-effects."

They played their usual games on the Play-Station Two and Jesse won as usual. She took his hand, he picked up a six pack of beer and a bag of chips, and they went back to the new bedroom that she had decorated. Life was good.

THE SPRING SPORTMEN'S CLASSIC of 2011was new to Jesse. He had never seen so many hunting and fishing toys, and grown men fondled them like girlfriend's breast. Jesse, Rufkin, and Otto arrived early. They were amazed at the different displays. Millions of product and dollars were being spent all for the purpose of killing some dumb animal, fowl, or fish. Too much money and time and too few alternatives.

The booths displayed testing of lures on live fish, films of killing big deer with bows, shoot-guns, and muzzle loaders. And movies of pheasants being blown into a pile of mush and feathers by crack-shot hunters. Both guards shook their heads. They had seen too much death to find this child's play interesting.

All three were dressed in jeans, camouflage shirts, and hunting hats. Both guards wore their camouflage coats loosely to hide their weapons and allow quick access. Their four-day-old beards and dirt covered boots allowed them to blend in like just another red-neck hunter. After moving all around the meeting area, they separated from Jesse and took up surveillance locations an hour before the scheduled meeting.

Jesse asked hundreds of questions to the experts about fishing and fishing boats. At first they ignored the scruffy hillbilly until he pulled out a wad of hundred dollar bills and asked if he could rent the boat. With that display, all the good-looking, charming salesmen were his new best friends. He loved playing with them. They showed him around for an hour and promised a free weekend trip to Lake of the Ozarks to try out their new 50 foot Cigarette Boat. He hated ending his game, took their cards, and promised to call them. Garcia and his men had arrived, ten minutes late.

Garcia looked around with obvious wonder. "You Americans waste a lot of money on trying to catch a few little fish. I think the real goal is to get out of the house, away from the wife, and act like big man."

Jess said, "You could be right. I never fished and never hunted. I just work and make money. I'm pretty simple."

"Stop with the simpleton act. You are a devious smart crook who has made a fortune and developed a marketing machine. Meet me in Cabo San Lucas for a week and I will entertain you and your leaders. I will explain our meth operation. We need to be partners."

"Garcia, do you think I'm fuckin' nuts? If I go to your place, I could never come back."

"I thought you might see it that way. I will pick you up in one of my Lear 55s at the Omaha airport. I will take you and all the guards you want. I will leave my wife and two sons with your team here in Iowa. They have always wanted to see farms and the west. If you don't come back, your team will have hostages. Here are copies of their passports. You can verify that the people who arrive are for real. I will not harm you, as I love my family."

Handshakes sealed the deal. The handsome, suave Garcia and the little rumbled hillbilly walked about all the displays and talked, like real friends. Garcia's head was never out of Rufkin's cross hairs as he lay motionless in the rafters.

SPRING HAD ARRIVED EARLY. Glen Oaks Country Club was open early in March. The maintance people covered in uniform Carthartt outdoor gear, scurried around at break-neck speed to remove the debris of winter.

Snyder sipped from a flask. "Scott we are crazy. I am freezing my aging, underutilized balls off. Why do you insist we play opening day? The wind is 30 miles an hour, the temperature is 45 degrees, and we are dressed like Eskimos playing golf."

"Snyder, stop wimping out! We can play nine and then go to my house to warm up. Valli has a new venture he wants to talk about."

The foursome finished with a total score north of 200 stokes, stinging fingers, and beet red cheeks. Opening day is a ceremony. Not necessarily a logical one.

Scott stopped by the Hy-Vee on 74th Street and bought four of their 12 ounce freshly cut Amana pork chops. Fielding swung by his home and popped his special pepperoni dip into the oven. Valli stopped by his home for a file.

Snyder showed up at Scott's home with a kicked hound look as his effort to get a date while buying several unique salads at Palmer's Deli had been rejected. The snicker from the young rejector had been very painful. His plans to test if he had any physical or mental side effects from the recent prostate surgery were again ruined. This time by a 30 year old female lawyer. A trip to Las Vegas to have a professional test the extent of his sexual recovery was becoming very high on his agenda. Professional sounds better than hooker.

After a couple of warm toddies, Valli threw the file on the table.

"We have a Mexican drug cartel which has unlimited access to pseudoephedrine, a key factor to make meth. The U.S. access is tight, but this material is made off shore. Quality control is merely a concept, not a practice. We also have a homegrown enterprising shit-kicker who provides virtually all the home grown pot markets in the Midwest. He has a marketing system that would put Avon to shame. He also has nearly unlimited access to farm fertilizer ammonia which is a key ingredient in meth. And easy access to propane for the heat necessary for production."

Valli paused for a sip and continued. "The two want to combine. They will make a mint. This combination will also fry thousands of brain cells in the poor slobs who think they can get a cheap escape without any consequences. "

Everyone stood in silence and looked at the pictures in the file of distorted faces on four young bodies. Their faces were twisted from the pain of too much meth. One of the faces was the child of the client providing the fee for this venture.

"The goal is to stop the merger. If the two leaders happen to disappear, that is a bonus but not a requirement. It is a challenge. We don't know where they are, or how to stop them. Otherwise the plan is pretty straight forward. Did I mention the ten million consulting fee?"

After a long silence and a deep sip of his hot toddy, Scott spoke up. "I am in. I need a change. Bad golf with no hopes of improvement makes me desperate for something new. My male ego is destroyed by my consistently regressing skills. I wondered if it was time to explore human growth hormones, especially one to repair diminished eye-hand coordination."

One by one the others agreed to this new geriatric vigilante adventure.

Scott said, "Let's call Walz and see if those drones he is trying to fly can do some surveillance work. Do we know where to start?"

Valli smiled. "My client believes the pot operation is located in Western Iowa. They have heard rumors of a little guy nicknamed The Lizard who runs the entire pot business. Rumors are he operates out of an underground cave. We know from paid informants that we are dealing with the Garcia cartel. They are one of the oldest cartels. They had their origins from several German Nazis who fled before Hitler's demise. Here is my file. Review it tonight, but no copies. If I am caught, I want no tracks leading back to you."

"By the way, I called Walz this morning. He will be flying the state locating construction jobs involving significant movement of soil. The heat sensors on the drone detect the varied temperatures of freshly moved dirt very easily. Snyder is there a way to determine if these projects are legitimate or off the books?"

Snyder popped out of his funk from being rejected by the good looking smart lawyer. He paused for a few seconds.

"Sure, there are several private computer systems used to advertise construction jobs and provide plans to bidders. In addition the Corp. of Engineers, DAS, DNR and DOT have computer files with the plans for their current projects. In addition, the various county extension operations might be tracking some projects. I just need to hack into their various computer systems to see what they have on file. If Walz gets me any suspicious locations, I can be into and out of their computer systems in a couple of hours. I think I can develop a system to open them all in sequence once I get into them for the first time. That would speed up future searches."

Fielding smiled. "I have been working on a couple of surveillance devices after talking with Walz and the drone humming bird story. There can be a lot of money in innovative surveillance equipment. I will move ahead on perfecting them. Ever think about rocks that can listen and birds that swivel their heads and act as electronic spies? I guess there is nothing wrong with a field test before the Patent process?"

CHAPTER FOURTEEN

"Listen, I Appreciate The Whole Seduction Thing You've Got Going, But Let Me Give You A Tip: I'm A Sure Thing."

JULIA ROBERTS - PRETTY WOMAN

✶✶✶✶✶

Initial merger meetings are typically disguised under non-invasive terminology; "let's get acquainted, let's see if our cultures are compatible, let's examine the level of our synergies and let's move slowly to determine if we have common goals." All of these high flying terms simply mean, "let's talk and see if we both can make more by being together, and how do we decide who will run the show when we are done!"

The white jet touched down at Omaha's Eppley Field on a blue bird clear late spring morning. Jesse was pleased to meet Kurt's family. The two small boys were between eight and ten years of age. Their black hair and coal brown eyes from their father, combined with a lighter hued skin tone, compliments of their Danish mother.

Liv Garcia was a six-foot tall blonde beauty. Her perfectly tanned skin and deep blue eyes were breathtaking. Her tight jeans and low buttoned blouse made it hard for Jesse to look her in the eyes and welcome her. With a few fumbling greetings, he handed the three Garcias over to Stella, who had a week of sightseeing planned in order to occupy their time while Jesse left for Mexico to negotiated the deal.

Jesse entered the narrow confines of the jet. He had never been on a plane before, let alone a private jet. His emotions ranged from scared-stiff to delighted as he felt the crushing power of the take-off and watched the land rush under him. He downed a couple of beers, relaxed in a plush tan leather seat, and watched the speeding panorama.

He had never realized how vast the United State's plains were until he watched for two hours as the green and gold below swept by him, from Iowa to Texas Land racing under the plane abruptly ended at the Texas border. The rushing transfer of brown Texas plains to the blue of the ocean at first sent chills of fear through him. This fear quickly changed to a mesmerized state of mind. He had never seen a lake bigger than Lake Okoboji in northwest Iowa, let alone an ocean. As the plane approached Cabo San Lucas, the water transformed into an azure blue color as it rushed up to meet the desert of the Baja.

"Boys, don't know what lies ahead. Keep an eye out. My instinct is we are okay as we have his family. Be careful to never split up and keep me in your sight. Let's watch what we drink and eat. Unless they eat it first, we don't touch it. Unless a fresh cap comes off in our view, we don't drink it."

Rufkin and Otto nodded and subconsciously touched the two Glocks and stilettos they each wore under their loose fitting shirts. They felt beads of sweat from fear pop out on their foreheads.

The trip from the private hanger at the airport to the tip of the Baja was fascinating. When they descended from the jet into the bright sun of Mexico, they were greeted by a black, stretch Lincoln limo with a driver who made Otto look skinny and weak. Jesse couldn't take his eyes off the biceps of the mastodon driver. Inside the limo were a car pocket of iced down Millers beer and a tray of freshly prepared deep fried tenderloins. Both were Jesse's favorites, but his suspicious mind allowed him to only have a beer.

"Hey, mister driver, want tenderloin sandwich? They look great!"

The driver smiled and shook his head. Jesse was instantly cautious.

Jesse's nose was pressed hard against the window in awe at the passing scenery. Rufkin and Otto were pivoting their necks to absorb the contrast that was on each side of them.

The four-lane highway was in perfect condition. It wandered down the coast line at the base of the coastal hills. On the left or west side was the azure-blue waters of the Sea of Cortez. Overlooking the sea, from the quickly ascending hillside, were opulent homes, golf courses, and hotels.

Jesse was non-stop in dispensing questions to Miguel, the driver. Miguel's English was quite good, likely better than Jesse's. He told them about each hotel, its owners, and its costs.

The golf courses intrigued Jesse. He had tried to watch the game on TV, but could not get into it for any period of time. He could not figure out what was so interesting about someone trying to put a tiny ball into a tiny hole. Even more confusing was how everyone in the crowd, and even the announcer, was so quiet until all of a sudden they would scream. Why not cheer, boo or trash-talk all the time? What a waste of time. No exercise. No contact. No players were ever happy. Pounding their clubs on the ground appeared to be the normal way to express anger. Why not throw the son-of-a-bitch at an opponent?

The east side of the car displayed a sight far more familiar to Jesse, stark poverty with people living a meager existence. Periodically the barren cactus-filled landscape would sprout a cluster of run-down houses, trailers, and rusting cars. The people in these clusters were very thin and wore rumpled torn clothes which presented a dramatic contrast to Miguel's spotless black uniform. The shops, garages, and grocery stores in these areas were decaying, rusting and in sad need of paint and repair.

Jesse noted to his guards, "Looks a lot like Southwest Iowa with cactus?"

The trip slowed as they entered the town of Cabo San Lucas. The streets were filled with shoppers milling around the numerous shops, the cafes and stores clean and new. In the harbor stood two tall, white cruise liners with a slight wisp of smoke rising from each of their three huge smokestacks.

He was awestruck. "I never knew a boat could be that big and still float. You could put Pisgah and Ute on its top deck and still have room."

The limo gradually slowed until they passed through a gate with a large steel fence and armed guards. It slowly proceeded up a steep hill by the large area sign announcing Pedregal. Jesse had given up on keeping track of the roads they had used to get to this steep hill that seemed to be composed of one large rock. His naturally nervous survival nature was in a high state of anxiety. Sweat filled the band of his John Deere cap and the pits of his denim shirt were soaked.

The limo, after a mile of climbing the winding narrow road, finally stopped. Above them balanced on a large stone crest was a rambling stone home that blended in perfectly with the landscape. Miguel went to the trunk and retrieved their three small DuPont Chemical logoed duffle bags. They, without a word, followed him up the 35 winding steps. When the three frightened souls crested the top of the stairs, they froze in awe as they gazed at the view.

In front of them was a cliff abruptly descending to the white sand below. On the horizon was a full panorama of the endless blue Pacific Ocean, broken only by an occasional white-capped wave, boat, or surfacing whale. To their left stood three giant, multi-colored hotels with pools at their base. Finestras, Capella and Playa Grande's sun loving patrons speckled the beach in colorful lounge chairs located in clusters near the crashing white surf. The towering rocks of El Arco at the far end of the long beach dominated the distant horizon, waves crashing high-up its jagged peak.

The Iowa visitors were all staring at the house.

Jesse softly whispered to his two body guards, "Never seen anything like this. Wonder what it cost? It's about as big as the Pisgah High School."

Rufkin and Otto were mute and shrugged as they unconsciously touched their hidden Glocks.

Miguel showed them into the main living area and took their bags. The room had a balcony over 400 feet long with a perfect view of the majestic horizon. It was filled with large metal sculptures that in some fashion all looked like bizarre forms of women. The numerous overstuffed chairs and couches were vividly colored red, yellow or blue. Each couch or chair had a table beside it with a glass top supported atop rocks that appeared to be the same color and texture as the brown granite stone floor.

"How do ya think they got the brown and gold streaks in the stone on that floor tile? Sure is a lot different than the floor in my cave." Jesse chuckled. He amused himself.

As they stood motionless, gawking around at the sexually explicit art on the walls, Kurt Garcia entered with two mammoth men behind him, each dressed in loose fitting, un-tucked black shirts flowing over brown trousers. Their guns were well concealed, but Jesse knew they were present and ready. They had to walk through the door one at a time because of their shoulder width.

Garcia himself was well over six-foot four inches tall. His dark, slicked back hair flowed down to his shoulders. His near-black eyes gazed through his thick eyebrows at Jesse. His tight lips parted with a perfect, but cold, smile displaying pearly white teeth.

"Welcome, Mr. Jesse. We have a lot to talk about. First we get to know each other. What is your drink preference? Miguel tells me you did not eat. Want to have something?"

"I would like a beer and a sandwich, but I would like one of your big boys to try part of it before I eat it."

"Jesse, my feelings are hurt. You have my dear family. I will guard your life with my own. Besides we are going to make millions together. Miguel, bring in a sandwich for my friends and one for me. I will take a bite of all four sandwiches to demonstrate that you they are safe."

When the sandwich arrived Kurt, true to his word, took a bite from all of the heaping sandwiches and took a deep swallow from the bottle of Pacifico before handing it to Jesse. They both smiled. Jesse quickly finished the sandwich and two beers.

"You are right in being careful. My father came to Mexico right after the war in Europe ended. He was German and was wanted by the Allied authorities. The Garcia name was adopted. He married my mother, God rest her soul, a few years after arriving. They were a beautiful couple. He brought money with him or had it in hidden bank accounts. He made an art of bribing local officials. His first fortune was made at smuggling liquor to the United States. He developed a small fleet of trucks and ships."

Garcia sat comfortably in a deep red-colored chair and gazed out at the blue sky and ocean. "I lived like a playboy in my early years. Papa Hans insisted on an English education, but he gave me plenty of money to enjoy my stay in London. On holidays, I found the French and Italian women especially unique. Their romantic instincts blended well with my devious German nature and my hot-blooded genes, complements of my mother."

Garcia hesitated as he stared at the endless Pacific view. "But, that all ended. Papa Hans was gunned down in front of our house, along with three guards. One guard was my childhood playmate, Fernando. I rushed home from London. I have long been broken hearted that I never really got to know my Father."

With a deep sigh and drink of Pacifico, Garcia continued. "At the funeral, we were all slowly walking from the gravesite when a gun-shot cracked. Mother fell dead at my feet. I went crazy for weeks try-ing to put the pieces together. After endless meetings with Papa Han's accountants, operations people, and lawyers, I figured it out.

Garcia sighed and continued with a grimaced look. "Hans had been talking to the Aviega family from Columbia about becoming involved in moving cocaine to the U.S. with our fleets. Turns out the Torres fam-ily did not want that to happen as it would disrupt a balance of power between the two families. The Torres appeared to be responsible."

Jesse cocked his head and in a quizzical voice, asked, "This family history is all very interesting, but how does it fit with this dumb hillbilly from Iowa?"

"Patience, my friend. There are two points to my story. Marketing, transportation and distribution mean everything in this world of drugs. People will pay a lot for them. That's why we need to be partners. The second point is you need to get to know me and my attitude about being deceived."

"After I discovered the cause of the death of my parents, I met with Juan Aviega and his key leaders. We worked out a market arrangement of sorts. I would give him access to my fleets. I also gave them the right to take over the Torres operation, if he could forcefully gain control of it. Juan, in turn, would give me complete control of the meth business in Mexico and the United States and they provided an endless supply of the key ingredient for meth, pseudoephedrine. You U.S. people find it in Sudafed or Contac."

Garcia leaned back in his chair and an evil tight-lipped smile came over his face.

"I next meet with Rico and Renaldo Torres and cut the same deal. Everyone was happy and thought they had won. That next weekend, the key leaders of the Aviega group and most of their families died on the same day. Seems they thought my Father could not be trusted, so they arranged to take over our family business after his death. Their effort to blame the Torres family was too obvious. Besides, the elimination of a competitor was good for the Torres group, and Rico understood the message to tread very carefully with my group. We have been great partners over the years."

Jesse tried not to sweat. He knew he was entering a new and complicated world. There was no turning back. He briefly told about his pot business and the way he operated. Garcia watched and listened intently.

"Before we end for the day, I want you to know that you can keep the pot business. I want the use of your cave. In fact, we will build more. I also want your sales system and the use of your transportation system. I will supplement your system with my sales teams, and we will control the sale of meth in the entire Midwest."

Jesse listened intently.

"Small towns are also our market, Jesse. These towns are free from close law control. The small-town people are all depressed from the economy that's dying around them. Often the ambitious ones work two jobs to make ends meet. They are tired and need energy. They need a happy rush now and then to help them cope with their otherwise depressing lives. Meth is the answer. It's quick, cheap, and available."

"Amigo Kurt, you have given me a lot to think about. I will have to take a little time to think as I'm not as smart as you. I really don't know much about this business, except I hear that shit is quick to hook the user."

"We will relax and not talk business anymore, my friend. You gather all your questions, and we will talk over the next few days as we get to know and trust each other. Right now I am going to introduce you to a Mexican legend, the LBLMs."

With a snap of his finger, the door opened and 10, nearly naked, beautiful Hispanic girls appeared. They were all thin, dark-haired, with seductive smiles displaying white perfectly formed teeth. Their dark skin was amply displayed because of their sheer black or red panties and bras. Jesse thought only a second of Stella. His second brain located deep in his jeans took control.

"May I introduce the LBLM, which is short for 'Little Brown Loving Machines,' my friend? You and your men can take your pick. They are here for the week. Don't be bashful. My two men will also join with you in a long afternoon and evening of relaxation. We dine at nine tonight. There are clean clothes and swimming suits in your rooms."

Jesse soon got over the shock. After a skinny dip in the pool overlooking the cliff with several LBFMs, he took two to his room. Rufkin and Otto did not join in and watched as Garcia's huge guards followed Jesse's example.

Jesse was at first embarrassed, but the soft hands and tongues of the three soon took dominance of his body. He never knew he could have sex with multiple people in so many ways. After a few hours he tired. Dressed in his new Tommy Bahama shirt, he went to the deck searching for a beer.

"Rufkin, give me your gun and knives. You go and enjoy yourself till you are tired. Then let Otto take a break."

Rufkin's stiff face broke with a smile as he handed his weapons to Jesse, and he shot into his bedroom after giving Jesse a hug, a kiss on the forehead and a long pumping handshake.

JESSE WAS TIRED, SATIFIED, AND CONFUSED. He melted into one of the six soft brown leather couches and tried to process the blizzard of facts that had just barraged him. As he slowly sipped on another ice cold Pacifico beer, a short, muscular, dark skinned lady in a nearly unbuttoned multi-colored blouse and white shorts entered the room at a rapid pace. Her six inch heels created a staccato rhythm on the brown marble tile. Her face was clearly European, not Hispanic, and the features were perfect. Her smile and flashing black eyes were seductive.

"Call me Carla. I am Kurt's chief assistant, and no, I am not another LBLM. Kurt wanted me to give you a little background on our merger and answer any questions now that you have relaxed."

He blushed, but could not take his eyes off of the most beautiful woman he had ever seen. Her eyes stared holes through him.

She sat down beside him. "Meth is the poor people's cocaine. The rich seldom get involved. It is cheap and can be made by anyone, although the qualities can vary. It is quite addictive, so the repeat sales are easy. It has been around for years. The German army had pills for long marches. Japan had plants producing it in mass to energize its dwindling army and navy. In fact, U.S. aviators had no-doze pills for long flights, fat people used it for dieting and many people use it for colds. The only difference is the potency level.

He listened intently. "How's it work?"

"In biochemical terms, it blocks the uptake of neurotransmitters. When you feel good from a physical action, endorphins or epinephrine are released into your brain. At that moment, you feel euphoria like you have just experienced a body pleasure, such as sex. Later the brain soaks up the released endorphins, and you return to a normal feeling. Meth blocks that return to normality for long periods and stimulates continued release by the brain. The brain dictates to the body to have endless energy, excited reaction, and an intense feeling of long term pleasure."

"Miss Carla, I understand it can be awful bad on ya."

"You are right. It is awful. Too much use creates an increasing need for more stimuli. People lose inhibitions, become paranoid, have delusions about the world around them and lose track of their lives. They stay up and work or play far beyond their bodies capacity. Their life span is incredibly shortened as lungs and organs are damaged, health habits are abandoned and their craving typically leads them to jail. No one in their right mind would ever use it if they understood the consequences."

He sipped his beer. "Wow. Why do you want to sell it?"

"It is a billion dollar a year profit center for us. We can make it here and use our fleet to get it to the States, but the costs would be reduced by huge measures if we had it produced and distributed locally. You're in the middle of the States. You are located perfectly for our first mega production and distribution center."

She moved slowly closer to him and handed him another beer. She slowly put a jewelry draped arm around him and casually passed her breast over his shoulder as she handed him the beer. He blushed.

"You and I will work together. I arrange for the installation of the manufacturing equipment, packaging, and chemists. You have to develop a bigger cave to house and maintain a fleet of cars, the tanks of anhydrous ammonia, and the mixing area. We cannot ship the ammonia component, which is a key ingredient, over long distances because it's in liquid form. So you need to acquire it by having local farmers over-order their fertilizer needs and stealing any extra needs from local farmers. We will get the Pseudoephedrine from our Asian source so you don't need to steal it from local drug stores. We have it manufactured in small factories all over Asia. Don't worry about how it gets into the States. You'll have all you need."

His mind was whirling as she softly took his hand and whispered, "We will be a great team. We have a lot of things to do together in the future."

By dinner he was exhausted. He tried some red wine and found he liked its taste. He even ventured and ate thick pieces of fish covered in a fruit sauce and enjoyed a salad with strips of a salty fish over it. He always waited until Garcia or Carla tasted each item before he ate. After a lot of meaningless talk about Iowa and his operation, he moved to the bedroom. Two LBLM's nuzzled next to him. After a couple of relaxing lessons in love-making, he asked them to leave, and fell into a fitful sleep filled with questions.

CHAPTER FIFTEEN

"Marriage Always Demands The Greatest Understanding Of The Art Of Insincerity Possible Between Two Human Beings."

VICKI BAUM - AND LIFE GOES ON

*****

Any successful acquisition or merger progresses slowly. Each side shows its cards one at a time, always being careful to determine if the real motive of merger is mutual benefit or conquer. When the parties have gotten comfortable with the concept that being one is better than being two, the poker playing process of determining terms commences. Some companies take the negotiating approach of starting at extremes and slowly moving to the middle. This process risks never finding the middle before a party gives-up and abandons the process. The better approach is to identify your terms, your rationale for requiring such terms, advocate the appropriateness of such terms and stand your grounds. Some flexibility is required, but working off your own agenda is the preferred route in this process.

After three days of talking about operations, sightseeing, great food, new wines, and fresh batches of LBLMs, Jess became tired, bored, and anxious. He knew he could not turn back. If he stopped, he was dead. If he went ahead, he was entering into a business that bothered him a great deal for some unidentified reason, as he had always been void of morality. He could not shake the fact that meth destroyed people. Pot just made them big, fat, and stupid. Natural greed was pulsating through his brain as was the thrill of doing another illegal act and profiting.

During dinner on the fourth night Jesse announced he had a proposal for them to consider, but wanted to make a few calls before he committed to anything. It was agreed that the next day they would stop all of the corporate courting and commence talking terms. After a couple of glasses of Argentine Cabernet, a big rib-eye steak, and a flaming Mexican banana dessert, Jesse excused himself.

He had just finished a call to Ted, the oldest and smartest Sharpe brother, and was making notes on his other calls when the door opened. His pencil dropped when he saw Carla standing nude in his doorway. Without a word, she took control, disrobed him and climbed on top. He hoped he did not look too shocked and intimidated while being made love to and controlled by a picture-perfect looking female who was stronger than him. Without much effort, he rose to the occasion and worked valiantly to make the visit mutually interesting. Thanks to several positions acquired from the LBLMs, he felt he had not disappointed his surprise visitor. Practice makes perfect.

When she finished her creative and energetic performance, with a slight kiss on the cheek, she glided out of the room.

"See you tomorrow, partner. We can have many wonderful times working together."

He was speechless. He knew he had just tasted another aspect of corporate seduction. He was more than a little angry, as he knew she believed that he was like many men, easily controlled with a little sex. While he enjoyed the process and planned to enjoy it again, he never lost sight of why it was happening. He was becoming a fast learner about corporate life and politics.

The morning sun came up like a huge orange ball emerging from the vast Pacific. Jesse sat in a balcony chair watching the beauty, sipping his deep black strong Mexican coffee, while nibbling on a muffin. He had been up before dawn.

At 9 am. Garcia, Carla and the guards entered the main living area. Coffee and pastries magically appeared. She was dressed in a white jump suit and multiple strands of gold jewelry. The two top buttons of her jumpsuit were unbuttoned to clearly display her cleavage. Jesse never looked at her. Rufkin and Otto were standing at the door to the entrance where Jesse sat looking calmly at the sunrise. Then he spoke in an unusually calm and precise fashion.

"Let's talk terms. You want me to triple the size of the cave under my hill. I will need six months, and about $500,000 in cash. I need to buy some construction equipment, wood, braces and other building components. I don't have time to steal it. I can have that part ready by spring."

Garcia smiled. "Done."

"I will need some real construction people to operate the equipment and build the interiors. The Sharpe boys are slow, and my pot is making them even slower. You also need to send up the equipment needed to kick off this operation. I'm just a dumb pot farmer and have no idea what to buy."

"Done. By the way, don't think that dumb pot farmer routine fools me." Garcia smiled.

"I will need at least a million dollars to keep my sales force happy till they have new product to sell. I intend to phase down the pot his fall and start training the guys to sell your product. I will need 50 used cars to give to them to keep them happy and to later use for making deliveries when the plant is up and operating."

"Done."

"I need a good sales person to help train Henry, my brother and sales director. He's never sold this shit before, nor ever managed this many people. We will need to have 10 English speaking Mexs with legal papers in the States in two months to start the training and market development."

Jesse glanced long at Garcia. "I want Carla there almost all of the time. I think she and I can be like peas in a pod and can really be a team."

She wiggled uncomfortably in her chair. She looked coldly at Jesse and his constantly swishing tongue. The Lizard's green-eyes stared intensely at her, looking all over her body. She knew she saw a smirk.

Garcia announced, "Done. Let's get started."

Jesse continued, "I have identified 30 towns in the west half of Iowa and east half of Nebraska where there are manufacturing plants using cheap labor: packing plants, turkey plants, egg plants and equipment manufacturing. Those small towns are dying and the workers are depressed and some working double shifts. They are the target. My guys will work the white boys and give them samples at a cut-rate cost or free. Your Mex's need to get hired and work on sales to the brown worker in order to suck them in. By the time our operation is ready, we will have all these markets begging for more product."

Garcia's eyes were blazing with excitement. "Done, but you will only need half that many Hispanics. The workers from Mexico don't waste their money on drugs; they send it to their families. They also have a strong cultural bias against these drugs. They have seen their effect on people. They aren't your real market."

Jesse never paused.

"I will need another $500,000 to help my poor farmer buddies buy the anhydrous ammonia fertilizer. They don't have much money, so we need to buy what they need for their crops and about a third more for our use. The co-ops will never figure it out, unless we buy too much for any one farmer. I will need a tank truck to go around and drain the product from the farmers' tanks and move it to our factory."

"Done."

"I also need to pay off my farm boys for having a smaller pot crop next year. I am going to tell them I am slowly quitting the pot business and taking up their farming income in a big way."

Garcia never blinked and, in fact, smiled. "Done."

"I need another million each month for the next six months to cover more security, some travel and to compensate me for the future loss of my pot business. After that we split the net fifty-fifty."

Garcia hesitated. "No. We keep 2/3 to cover our costs of procuring the pseudoephedrine, the transportation, and our people. You pay for the costs of your people. The money demands are okay. I have three duffle bags packed with enough cash to cover your costs and prepay the first three months to show good faith."

Jesse stared up into Garcia's deep brown eyes. His green-eyes never flinched. His tongue was in constant motion.

"Throw in a small jet like yours and a pilot when I need it, and we have a deal."

Garcia motioned no with his hand. The kitchen door opened and a bubbly wine on ice that Jesse had never tasted was delivered to everyone by the new group of LBLMs. Jesse never smiled, outwardly. He thought, I got to tell Stella about this deal. He reconsidered, well not everything! He allowed a small smile to cross his lips as he sipped his champagne with a LBLM in his lap giving him a farewell present!

Abruptly Jesse jumped up leaving the LBLM and walked to his room to pack. He was ready to go home. He missed it. He missed its solitude. Maybe, he also missed Stella?

CHAPTER SIXTEEN

"That Married Couples Can Live Together Day After Day Is A Miracle That The Vatican Has Overlooked."

BILL COSBY

*****

As companies merge, the process of unfamiliar people learning to work together is an enormous hurdle. In this process, the future pecking order for power is the underlying and unspoken issue in every meeting. Rarely is the common good of the respective shareholders even a factor. The second unspoken issue is that some people will become expendable and must be eliminated. Companies during this post-merger process try to guise the issues of power and survival under high flying labels. The reality is that it is a destructive, frustrating process and the sole issue is personal survival. Managing that process is an unenviable task.

The plane ride to Omaha was uneventful. After touchdown, Stella and the Garcia family greeted Jesse. Liv and both boys had on Hawkeye tee shirts.

"You have a lovely state. Stella was a wonderful tour guide. She drove us all around. We saw Okoboji and played in the amusement park. We visited the Grotto, your capital buildings and your historical museum. The boys loved playing cowboys in your beautiful hills. You have a gem in Stella. She is so considerate and kind. You look like you enjoyed your trip. Your beard is gone, your hair is cut and your clothes are right off of a GQ magazine."

Jesse did not know what GQ was, but guessed it was a compliment to the new clothes Carla had picked out for him. The fresh haircut and shave were also her ideas. As he looked at Stella who was getting big hugs and kisses from the departing Garcias, he felt a new feeling **:GUILT!** He was not sure how to deal with this new emotion.

The ride to the cave at Pisgah was quiet. No own spoke. They all looked at the jutting bluffs of the Loess Hills as they followed I-29 to the Little Sioux exit and drove the back roads towards Pisgah.

As they swung into the cave with the new black GMC Denali, which Garcia had left as a gift, all three silently looked at each other. He reached into the duffle bags and counted out $20,000 dollars for Rufkin, Otto, and Stella.

"Guys thanks for keeping me safe. Stella, thanks for baby-sitting with the Garcia kids. We have a lot of work to do. You will be busy but well paid. Just keep on keeping me safe!"

Stella hugged him after the two guards had left. He again felt that new emotion, guilt.

She held him tight. "I missed you. I want to hear everything."

He walked into the cave's kitchen, grabbed a cold six-pack of Millers, a bag of chips and her hand.

"I realized on the plane trip, I missed you. The sunset is going to be beautiful and the moon will be full and bright. Let's walk up the hill and talk. I may be over my head. The meth deal with the Garcias has me confused. If I say no, I am dead. If I go ahead, I am building a business that will kill or retard people. On the other hand if I go ahead, I will make a fortune. Life used to be simple."

He looked long at the setting sun as it was slowly falling into a cloud bank over the Missouri River. The billowing cumulous clouds were gradually taking on the appearance of a bonfire with moving, changing, colors of red and yellow.

"I know if I go ahead, they will eventually eliminate me and put their own people into control. I am being used as an easy way to transfer the business to them. When that's done, I am as valuable as yesterday's newspaper."

With a long gaze at the horizon, he looked long at Stella. He reached for her hand.

"Their people will come here and be our best friends and pals. What will really happen is they will be here to learn our business and eliminate us one at a time. We are just like those people in the paper, where that Des Moines seed company was recently taken over by an East Coast chemical company. After two years, all of the leaders are grazing in the field watching someone new fuck up their business."

"Jesse, there is no turning back. We have to think of a way to get our friends out of this with some money and a future. I can't live, building a company that will fry the brains of a bunch of poor depressed people who don't know better." Stella gave him a short kiss on the cheek.

After he returned to Pisgah, events moved at a rapid pace. Within a week Garcia's people arrived and started the process of developing the new operation. They talked to him about mutual interest, working together, learning from each other, and growing together. This "blending of cultures" language was textbook in execution. But in reality, as always, it was a guise to take over control of the entire business in a series of small but defined steps.

Three structural engineers arrived from Mexico City. Jesse was careful to make sure they were not too conspicuous to nosey locals. They were dressed in jeans with dirty winter coats to protect them from the cold winds and make them appear like locals. Every day, as they arrived, they drove old pickups through the tree covered north entrance to the hill containing his warehouse cave. The pickups were carefully hidden under camouflage canvas.

The engineers designed a football field size cave located under the round hilltop. The east quarter would be sealed off by explosion-proof walls. This would be the production area containing the anhydrous ammonia, mixing vats and drying area. The center portion would contain a garage for the fleet of vehicles and a repair shop. The west quarter would contain several offices and a training center. This area would have a well concealed, one-way, bullet-proof window looking south down the slope to the pastoral view below, the only unobstructed approach route. The other less obvious approach routes to the north would have several additional security cameras, motion detectors, and hidden sniper locations installed.

The north exit route from the cave complex ran down the heavily treed hidden side of the hill containing the cave. The road was covered with deep layers of gravel that would allow access in any weather. Trees and bushes were planted in the road to cause it to further blend in to the hills.

The building plans were presented to Jesse and the Sharpe brothers. Jesse was in awe, and again realized, he and his team were being slowly consumed. The Sharpe brothers were speechless as they knew this work would take years to perform. They were relieved when the head engineer announced that thirty workers would arrive in a week to start the process. The engineers even took over the task of renting equipment and procuring building material.

Jesse was careful to force the engineers and new workers to avoid detection from nosey locals. All of the equipment and material was delivered by trucks to a meadow five miles from the work-site. He and the Sharpes delivered it at night to the cave area and stored it in a heavily treed area where it could be accessed as needed.

By early June, the cave entrance had been built and camouflaged. Half of the new cave had been excavated and steel beams were placed to support the sides and top. Jesse stood back and let the energetic Hispanic crew work their twelve-hour shifts. The Sharpe brothers showed up when they felt like it and were given menial tasks to occupy them. They didn't mind as they were becoming progressively alcoholic and pot addicted.

The money to pay for the workers, equipment, material and fixtures didn't come directly to Jesse as he had discussed. Garcia simply had the items paid for. Jesse knew control was slowly being taken from him, but the million a month payments did arrive, so he said nothing. Stella routed the money to off-shore banks that some of her relatives had used to move money out of Europe during their civil war. She always consulted with him and only the two of them had the key numbers to facilitate a transfer.

The culture blending process was completed. The old culture was lost, changed or forgotten and the new culture was in total control. That's the way mergers work from Wall-Street to Pisgah, Iowa.

VALLI AND SCOTT quietly ordered a drink at Pal Juans, one of their preferred watering holes. "Templeton Rye for me," Scott said.

We don't have any rye or any bourbon, big shot" hissed the long haired bearded bartender.

"What do you have then, dipshit?" Scott snapped as his German-Irish temper flared.

"We got red wine; it's not good, but it's red. Want to sniff the twist off cap asshole?"

Scott turned to Valli. "What is this jerk doing working here?"

Just then the bartender stumbled, skidded, and caught the glass of red wine just as it was about to spill on Scott's newest St. Croix sweater.

"Good to see you again, Scott. I understand you need some good PI help?"

Jock Tenny slowly removed his beard and mustache and began to laugh. His gap-toothed Teddy Roosevelt-like grin made it obvious it was Jock. Jock had been making a good living throughout the Midwest being a PI to anyone who could afford him. He worked divorces, corporate white collar crimes, and union avoidance and bank fraud cases. He had been a long time friend of Scotts who often used him on discrete projects. He was beyond words valuable for spotting a group that were about to unionize or to arouse a group that was dissatisfied with a union. He also could find an employee engaged in embezzlement in a short period. Companies periodically hired him to come in to do a review for employee theft. He often took the cases on a contingent arrangement.

Tenny was at heart a frustrated actor who had performed in the Des Moines Play House in a dozen roles. He prized the pictures of himself in various get-ups especially Professor Harold Hill from Music Man and the Tin Man from Wicked. He loved the art of disguise.

Scott sipped his red wine. "Valli obviously called ahead. We have a job. We think we have located a large pot operation. It is expanding and going into meth. We need to know if we have the right location and when the kick-off of the operation will be. We want to know who the key operator is, what he looks like, and where to locate him? Did I mention he is very dangerous? So twice the normal rate covers the risk factor?"

Jock smiled and nodded. "I just separated from my 37 year old live-in. She found that my falling asleep by ten and farting during the night wasn't attractive. So I have a lot of time. Where am I going?"

Scott set the plastic wine glass down. 'You are right. This is bad wine, or did you give me vinegar? What week this month was it made? To answer your question, ever hear of Pisgah, Iowa?"

CHAPTER SEVENTEEN

"I Either Want Less Corruption, Or More Chance To Participate In It."

ASHLEIGH BRILLIAN

*****

The process after a merger occurs is one of the more interesting eras in a business cycle. The acquired company's people busy themselves teaching their new partner about their methods, cultures,, and values. The acquirer's people talk in terms of mutual respect, long term relationships, and unlimited cooperation. Unfortunately, the acquirer's people are under orders to learn as much as possible, as fast as possible, in order to eliminate as many of the acquired companies people as possible. It's called synergy.

Jesse had watched the building process near completion. He had busied himself by educating his pot growing farmers about their new subsidy. He first announced to them, one on one, that he was getting out of the pot business. He then relieved their sorrow when he told them about a new subsidy that was even better.

The farmers would buy their anhydrous ammonia fertilizer as usual, but they would order one-third more than they needed. Jesse would provide them with cash on a monthly basis in so that they could gradually pay the co-op. Full payment up front would be suspect as these farmers were traditionally on the overdue payment lists. They were advised that without warning on any given night, a fertilizer tanker would arrive and he would pick up the extra fertilizer.

The farmers were all smiles when he left. They nodded when he reminded them to keep quiet as each was the only farmer with this deal and he still had pictures of their pot farm.

To even further align the farmers to the operation, Carla delivered to each of them a perfumed-smelling note which contained an invitation to Minnie's Cafe, in Omaha, for dinner and a night of sex. Each received a picture of the same curvy blonde tart that would be their date for the evening. Minnie was very efficient and professional in keeping them scheduled on different days, feeding them well, and screwing their socks off. She was also careful to take good pictures and DVDs of their performances.

Carla accompanied Jesse to all of the farmer suppliers. Her well built body and beautiful face immediately attracted the attention of the farmers. Although they tried to be stoic in not drooling, their fumbling talk gave them away. Carla was careful to have her Carthartt coveralls unzipped low enough to show off her ample cleavage.

After an initial visit, she returned and delivered the cash to each farmer, ran through the deal again, and showed them their pictures with Minnie. They each went pale over the picture, but accepted another invitation to dinner with Minnie. Carla now was in control of the inventory source.

Henry had an extremely productive year. He had expanded the sales force throughout Iowa and Nebraska. No small town was uncovered. The Avon pyramid formula was, as usual, very powerful and quick to implement. He had also personally visited each of his ex-pot dealers and had given them an unexpected cash bonus. He had also educated them on the new product, delivered a few samples to distribute free or cheap to future customers, and gave them a stern lecture.

"Don't you pot heads ever use this shit. It will mess you up. You will become stupid and likely fired and in jail before you know it. This stuff is trouble. It's okay if you sell it but don't use it, even just as a sample."

All the lazy pot head small-town boys would nod like bobble-head dolls. Henry knew at least half would be fired or jailed and hopelessly hooked within six months of the introduction of the new product line.

Carla had unlimited energy. Besides overseeing construction and meeting the farmers, she spent the spring riding with Henry and meeting the sales force. She only met with the area director. She would take them to dinner, drink them silly, and flirt with them. They always gave her their lists of names and address of the sales people in their area with the hopes of getting laid by her the next time she returned. There was no doubt in Henry's mind they would get screwed, but not laid.

By late June, Carla, in her sexiest jeans and see-through black blouse, again visited the area directors. This time she was accompanied by Martin Garcia, Kurt's second cousin. Martin was half Mexican and half Swedish. The results of this unique combination produced a huge body like a Viking, blue eyes and extremely dark tanned skin topped by shoulder length blonde hair. He struck a menacing picture. His English was perfect and delivered with a very soft voice. He stressed production, no theft of money or product, and his strong desire not to ever need to replace them. His cold long glare, after referring to replacing them, sent a shiver through each of them.

As they departed, Martin always gave each a bear hug, a long stare and a knuckle crushing handshake. Each froze when he smiled a villainous smile and said, "Don't disappoint me. I like you and would miss having you around."

Carla would follow Martin and whispered, in each ones ear, "Work hard and be careful."

Even the dumbest pot-headed farm boy understood the rules had changed. They also knew that failure or dishonesty were not options.

HENRY AND JESSE disappeared from their work one late summer day and walked to a meadow three miles from Jesse's cave complex. They sat down in silence and looked for long silent periods of time at the meadow with its emerging prairie grass and budding prairie flowers. The sweet smell of living growing plants provided a soothing fragrance relaxing them like a tranquilizer. The deer, pheasants, and turkey casually walked around them as if they were part of the landscape. Life was simple here.

"Jesse, we are dead or in jail if we stay with the operation. We are dead even if we tell them we are leaving. What's you think?"

"You have it figured right. They now control inventory, sales and production. We are like stale bread to them."

Jesse leaned back, gazed at the cloudless blue sky and pulled a Millers and a Coke from his knapsack.

"I think you should grab a bag of money, take the best pick-up in the fleet and disappear right before they kick off production. I have a card from the best plastic surgeon in Minneapolis to get a new face for you. This time, not ugly, but pretty. Pay him in cash. Then rent a house in the Gull Lake area and blend in with your new face. It's a couple of hours north of Minneapolis and has a lot of tourists in season and no one after October. You can simply disappear among them. Just fish, hunt, play, or work. But stay legal and sober."

Jesse sipped his Miller and said, "Until I get there and we plan our new lives, you need to be smart and stay below the radar. You have enough money to last a long time. In the bag I gave you yesterday is a throw-away cell phone, a new passport using the name Harvey Morris, honorable discharge papers, social security card, college transcript, three credit cards and a Minnesota driver's license. The throw-away phone has my private throw-away phone number attached. Stella and I are the only ones who have your number."

Henry gazed for several minutes at the sky and chewed on a wild oat stem. "We really don't have a choice, do we? Will you be along sometime? How about Stella?"

"I expect to join you with Stella and her new face, but it won't be easy. I have sort of a plan. I do, however, want to take one more trip to Cabo and visit those LBLMs one more time and get a few more bags of cash."

HIGH OVER HEAD THE ANCIENT DRONE WAS CIRCLING. Walz was on another of his training exercises. The rumors of a new manufacturing location had been easily located. Several cruises of the drone at 30,000 feet around the Midwest had located hundreds of earth-moving projects. Snyder's skilled use of the computer quickly provided official plans that described the legally approved projects. All projects were legitimate except for the one in the Loess Hills near Pisgah. No plans were on file. The movement of dirt was large. Even the best efforts to conceal it in the Loess Hill's valleys failed. The sensor on the drone focused on the uneven temperature created by freshly unearths soil. The heat from many cooling pickup motors in the area was easily detected through the camouflage covers.

Walz called on the private cell phone. "Valli, take down these coordinates. We are set. I will come back tomorrow and take another look. I am sending Snyder the pictures, I just took. He can compare them to the ones I take tomorrow to determine that there is really construction going on or if they are done."

Walz said, "Well my friend, I need to get this damn old slow drone home. I am nearly out of fuel and this could be my last wreck as this is the last of the old drones they will let me play with."

"I am starting my advanced humming bird drone training tomorrow. They all have names. I have Harriet I. Hope she has a hard shell. My big hands are not very nimble with that joy stick."

Valli paused, "If you handle it like your putter, no one is safe."

The cell phone went silent.

CHAPTER EIGHTEEN

"You Can Only Milk A Cow So Long. Then You're Left Holding The Pail."

HANK AARON

✳✳✳✳✳

Every CEO or key officer in a merger needs to be realistic. The bigger, stronger partner always takes control. Part of control is to remove all the old power holders and replace them with people blindly loyal to the company. The idea of blending culture and keeping leadership in place are words from a textbook and not from the heart. Good exit planning dictates that the victims see the results coming and plan ahead.

Jesse called Garcia. "I need to meet with you in Cabo. There have been a lot of changes, and we need to discuss the future."

Garcia's jet arrived in Omaha the next day. Jesse, Rufkin and Otto were instantly off to Cabo. This time they were kept waiting for two days until Kurt returned from a sudden emergency. They filled the days by walking through the streets, eating unusual meals, and haggling with the beach vendors. One day they even went Marlin fishing. All three got sea sick as soon as the horizon disappeared. They took turns fishing, throwing-up and drinking beer. All concluded this would be the last Marlin trip. Fishing for bass, carp and bullheads in the local rivers didn't make you puke your guts out.

At late afternoon, the LBLMs would arrive, and they exhausted themselves by dinner time. They would then walk down the hill into town, with a post-sex smile etched on their faces. They discovered the Giggly Marlin, Cabo-Wabo, and Squid Roe. While they drank beer and ate fresh shrimp, they laughed at the sights. Every young visiting male was in tight jeans wiggling around to the rhythm of the music and grabbing his crotch every thirty seconds. Bevies of female in varied sizes, color, and shape would also arrive by mid-evening, dressed in ultra-tight jeans, and either a bright colored small halter top or a see-through blouse.

The three observers never danced as they didn't know how. They never flirted, as they had their testosterone tanks drained by the LBLMs every morning and afternoon.

Jesse was delighted when word came that Garcia would be two days late. Jesse knew he was keeping him waiting to check on how the takeover was working and to show him who was boss. Jesse didn't mind the power game. He took his time and enjoyed the wine, the food and the LBLMs. Rufkin and Otto, however, became intensely careful and anxious.

When Garcia arrived, he stepped out of his limo with his two hulking guards dressed in their customary black garb. It appeared to Jesse that they had all added 20 pounds of bulging muscle.

"Well, my amigo, good to see you. You have done well. You are a man of your word. I trust all of your money arrived on time?"

"It did. You, too, are a man of your word."

After a couple of drinks on the deck overlooking the endless waves, Jesse gathered his nerve.

"I know your people are running everything and I am okay with that. My people are way over their heads in this deal. Your people are much better equipped to run everything going forward."

"Jesse, it is good that you see things realistically, and won't resist these changes. Where does this leave us?"

"I would like a severance package for me, Henry, Stella, the three Sharpes, and my two guards. And the chance to quietly leave. I found a place in North Dakota where there are lots of fish, deer, pheasants, and pot-heads. Thought I would just move there and do it all over again. Maybe you can come buy me out again?"

"How much, and how soon?" Garcia's eyes narrowed.

"I was thinking two million for me and a half-million for each of the others. I will leave when you want."

"Done. Half the money will arrive in a week. The day after the plant kicks off full operations in high gear you can leave. The other half will be delivered to you when I know that all is going well in the transition."

"I think that's fine. Your word is good enough for me."

Garcia stood, shook hands, and quietly spoke. "We have some bad news. There was a cave-in this morning and the Sharpe brothers are dead. They won't be needing their severance pay." He faked a sorrow-ful look, and then left without a word.

Jesse knew he was dead when the plant kicked off its operations.

After two more days of wine, food, and LBLMs, the three returned to Pisgah. They each had a smile tattooed on their face, and agreed what had happened in Cabo stayed in Cabo.

A good negotiation for severance and retirement leaves everyone feeling good. The follow-through is where the problems emerge.

ON A BLUFF OF THE LOESS HILL overlooking the work walked two turkey hunters. They were obvious. Their orange vests stood out against the greening hills. They each were carrying a turkey. To the naked eye the turkeys looked real, not just rubber decoys.

"Well Valli looks like we have Fielding's mini-cameras in place and the listening devices pointed in the right direction. No one will figure out that those fake blackbirds and sparrows are packed full of such great visual equipment. It's ingenious how they periodically move and flap a wing. Turning their heads is a nice touch, plus it expanded the range of vision from the bird's eye cameras."

Valli tapped the Blue-Ray in his right ear. "Scott, lets head east away from here on a casual but steady pace. Fielding just called and reports his cameras show three guys walking up the ridge towards us. I don't want to get to know them."

When the two got to the car, they turned on the computer and went to the website Snyder had activated exclusively for the use of the cameras. They watched from the varied bird's eyes as the three hillbillies wandered around looking for signs of trespassers. The piles of two turkey entrails and feathers were convincing.

Scott packed the car with unusual haste. "I need to get home by seven. I am on my third date with this foxy lady who just moved to Des Moines. She has moved from Forest City and has a great condo at the Point at Glen Oaks. Her kitchen is right out of Architectural Digest, the living room has the best of old world furniture from Trieste and I hope to explore the bedroom tonight. We have had three dates and I thinks it's time to determine if sex is a reality or a memory in her mind. I know where it stands in my mind."

"Scott, you amaze me. You are always getting hot for someone only to dump them. You really need to move on. Terri has been gone now for four years. But, all I can say is best of luck. I hope all your rusty equipment works and you don't disappoint her. By the way tell me more about this new object of your decaying lust."

"Unfortunately you are right. I am not sure someone can ever really love twice. But Jane is nice. She lost a husband to cancer so we have the care-giving thing in common. She just moved here from Forest City. Apparently she went on a cruise alone last fall and rediscovered a need to look ahead and try new roads on that old map of life. I guess I am one of the first new roads. I am not sure if she views me as an Interstate or a worn out farm to market road."

The trip back to Des Moines was quiet. "Valli, what do we do next? We know where the site is being built, but we don't know when it is to kick off. We also aren't sure when or if the two owners will ever be together."

Valli winked. "I think it's time Tenny earns his pay. Want to tag along as his side-kick and get to know the latest news from the 300 residents of Pisgah?"

CHAPTER NINETEEN

"Nobody Ever Forgets Where He Buried The Hatchet."

KEN ABE MARTIN

*****

The process of leaving a company that has been built by its founder and his team is emotionally complex. The reality of knowing they will not see it grow, will not control its direction, and will no longer control its workforce, causes deep emotional wounds. The loss of control is a blow to any ego. These realities must be accepted. Such results were inescapable from the day the merger courtship commenced. A smart leader follows the example of General MacArthur and, like a good old soldier, quietly walks away.

Jesse brought Henry, Stella, Rufkin and Otto to his office at the west end of the underground facility. He solemnly handed them a portion of the first installment of their severance. He brought from Cabo in Pioneer-logoed gym bags. It was nearing the end of summer and the operations needed to be kicked off.

"Don't expect the other half. When the time is right I will give you some directions and new identities. We have to disappear, but we need to be able to get a hold of each other. Stella's working on that plan."

He took a deep breath of the humid summer air. "The Sharpe brothers' death was odd. They were found early one morning crushed and smothered in a wing of the excavation where the ceiling bracing was being installed. Their bodies had been returned to their few family members with a story about them going off the cliff west of Pisgah and falling to their death, drunk and high. No one doubted the story as those boys were high more days than they were sober. I doubt the story. There's no way those boys would be working that early in the morning. They would still be hung over."

As the opening days operations neared, tempers erupted among Garcia's people as deadlines were missed and fingers pointed. Jesse just chuckled and watched.

AS THE LONG HOT DAYS OF SUMMER PASSED, Jesse busied himself with staying visible with all the Garcia leadership. He took Carla on one last visit with the farmers to assure her that they would provide plenty of anhydrous ammonia. They also visited all the area sales leaders.

Unfortunately, it was obvious to him that one-third of the sales leaders had been sampling the product. Sniffling noses, running eyes, jittery actions, and endless energy oozed from the culprits.

While Jesse and Carla were driving back from a long trip, he, with an impish look, abruptly put his right hand on one of her ample breasts with a firm squeeze.

"Let's spend a night at the Council Bluff's casino. We haven't enjoyed a little sport sex in a long time. Besides, I want to tell you about my new guys in Wisconsin that want to become area sales managers."

Her first reaction was a telltale flinch as she pulled away from the small hand that tightly held her left breast. But she quickly smiled and they headed towards Council Bluff. She was always ready for a little sex for profitable information.

After a few drinks, a good steak, and some bad blackjack, they went to the room hand in hand.

She entered the room and opened two mini-bar vodka containers. She swallowed each of them in a single gulp. She then mechanically and systematically removed Jesse's clothes and prepared him for the night's treat.

He was amused. He noted the non-stop work and fattening Iowa food had added ten pounds to her normally trim frame. But he enjoyed every minute of her emotionally void performance because he knew she wasn't enjoying it.

He tried every move and position that the LBLMs had taught him. After awhile, he thought he noticed that Carla might actually be enjoying the process, although he wasn't sure as she was a great actress. Her moans, groans, wiggles and gasps were perfectly timed to trick any lover into feeling successful and very masculine.

After a great performance, she asked for details on the Wisconsin lead. Jesse rambled on inventing names and places as best his limited geography knowledge would allow.

"After we get open, I will take you up to Racine and we can get started. My friend says he has a brother in Fargo who will follow suit. I think a road trip together for several nights would be great? How about you?"

She tried valiantly to hide the revulsion and shock at the thoughts of screwing the little Lizard a few more times. Although his energy and style was impressive, he was still thin, homely, and often dirty. His limited education and vocabulary left little to do after sex was over. Oh well, that's part of the job, she thought. Hope my bonus from Garcia makes it worth the effort.

"Sure sounds great. I have never seen Wisconsin or North Dakota."

SCOTT AND VALLI returned a few days to the site of their fake turkey hunt. Under cover of night, they went to the high ridge following the lighting devices they had dropped the day before. Fielding's new technology made the rock-like devices emit lights visible only through special lenses added to conventional night vision goggles. They had to move quickly as the lights had only eight hour life remaining before they automatically disintegrated into a ground pile of dust.

They quickly slid the small rocket launcher into the fabricated hollowed out log and threw grass and molding leaves over it. Sighting it on the center of the cave and the main door at night was no problem, as Snyder fed them the coordinates that he had previously prepared using the cameras from two of the blackbirds. The triggering, which would be fired by a cell phone call, was activated.

Now the only questions were when the merger candidates would arrive and when was the optimum time to fire the rocket? The surveillance equipment and Walz's occasional drone flyover made it clear the work was nearly done. The large warehouse door was installed and camouflaged to perfectly blend into the hill. The bird's eye cameras revealed large boiling vats and ammonia tanks arriving daily.

On the trip back Scott finally blurted out, "I know you are not asking about my visit with Jane in case it was a bust."

Scott could not handle the silence. "By the way, her bedroom is very sensual. It's all white carpet, a fancy multicolored bedcover with piles of pillows, and a great shower built for two. The big screen TV should be great if I ever have time to watch it. I may have discovered a woman who can make me think I am 18 again. Well, at least twice I thought I was 18."

THE PLAN WAS SET. The flaw was that no one knew when the key players would arrive, if they ever would arrive, and when the operation would kick off. Fielding had a solution.

Lucas did a low evening flyover of the site. The sound of the props of the drone was hardly audible. From the belly of the drone dropped 50 rocks that fell indiscriminately around the cave. Inside the rocks were small listening devices that transmitted to a booster site installed in one of the observation birds which directed any noises to Fielding's computer in Des Moines. The computer was voice-activated to avoid listening to hours of silence.

Scott and Jock were on their way to determine what the citizens of Pisgah knew about their new industrial complex. They entered Pisgah in a tired Old Home Bread truck. The 18 wheeler was faded and black smoke bellowed from its smoke stack because of the aged oil rings in the diesel motor. The worn-out mufflers could be heard for two miles away.

Even though the bread company had long been gone, it was always remembered in Pisgah because of the short lived convoy type of commercials. Jock with his charm was dressed like a movie executive in a blue blazer, white pants, straw Panama hat and cigarette holder. Scott was the driver. They entered the run-down café that was the original Old Home Filler-Up Café.

"This is perfect. Anyone here ever appear in those Old Home Bread Commercials?"

One hand went up. "My great uncle was the boy friend of Mavis. Does that count?"

"No, but nice try, son. We are going to shoot some remakes of those commercials because the company is coming back to life. Anyone here want to apply for a role?"

Within an hour Jock had interviewed 20 people. His charming manner and gap-toothed grin had everyone talking to them. He had three phone numbers from buxom locals who knew a private interview would seal their role. He also had five guys who knew they could do the driver role. He had three people sing the theme song for him. He also found that a young guy named Jesse Marvin was the owner of a large pot operation three miles west of town. He was rich and feared. The extremely buxom cafe owner volunteered she had a big order from Jesse, a lot of booze and food scheduled for next week.

After three hours, Scott drug Jock to the truck. It was time to leave. Jock argued his case that his private interviews with the aspiring actresses could clearly provide more information. He needed to stay the night. Jock lost. The antique truck sped out of town. Black smoke bellowed as Scott put the pedal to the metal.

Jock was humming and singing a few verses. "Come on up Rubber Duck, there's no Smokies ahead or behind. We got ourselves a convoy."

"Shut up Jock. You did better doing 76 Trombones."

VALLI WAS NOT satisfied with the details. He was a stickler for a foolproof plan. Fielding's listening rocks proved their worth as they provided various scraps of Mexican phrases from the cave site. There were references to the arrival of Jaffe Garcia and his sexy assistant, a jet to Omaha, a celebration, big bonuses, and returning to their homes. There were also references to Marvin, The Lizard, and two body guards whose size and dark looks scared the workers.

The project was done and about to kick into production. He knew the plan required more precision. It must look like a cave-in. Timing needed to be perfect to eliminate the leaders.

Snyder came up with the idea of placing a bug into the FAA system to immediately report to any non-commercial jets that filed a flight plan to Omaha, Lincoln, or Des Moines. The system would flash a warning from his computer to his I-phone when a flight plan was filed.

Valli knew from years of experience that waiting was always the best practice. The prey would soon reveal themselves. All he had to do was drive to western Iowa at the right time, watch the cave through the eyes of the birds, and make a phone call to the rocket.

IN THE QUIET OF THE EVENING, Stella and Jesse planned out their escape. They set up signals and timetables. They created new identities for everyone complete with passports, credit cards and social security numbers. They laid out directions to the location of three safe houses Jesse had purchased and equipped several weeks before. They obtained secret cell phones and gave them numbers that would allow access on an as needed basis between Henry, Rufkin, Otto and themselves. They gave Henry a Pioneer duffle bag with $300,000 dollars and he silently disappeared after a long hug from Jesse.

The timing for the plan was close at hand. The need to eliminate Garcia and Carla was obvious. If they lived they would never stop until all of them were dead. A couple of blocks of military plastic explosives under one of the ammonia tanks would resolve the issue. Rufkin quickly provided the blocks of explosive and a detonator that could be activated by Jesse's phone from over a mile away.

He new the best place for the explosive was in the middle of the propane and ammonia tanks. The impact would be devastating. In his westerly portion of the cave the impact would be hardly felt because of the protective walls he had engineered into its design.

The idea of killing Garcia and Carla did not bother him. They were void of any concern about the damage their product inflicted. It was just business. The death of the laborers and engineers did bother him. They were just earning a living for their families without any profit from the sale of the meth. He finally lost his temporary pang of guilt. They were collateral damage.

Female Dominance: Will I Know It When I See It?

****

PART THREE

"Lipstick Isn't Just Sexy. Lipstick Is Power."

BARBARA FOLLET

CHAPTER TWENTY

"Men Are Only As Loyal As Their Options"

BILL MAHER

✷✷✷✷✷

KURT GARCIA GRADUALLY awoke as the heat from the morning sunrise ushered in another sweltering day at Cabo San Lucas. He raised his head, partially opened his near black eyes, and ran his fingers through his course, shoulder-length graying black hair. The sun glowed like a Coppertone ad on his sharply chiseled bronze face. The ancient Mexican Indian genes of his mother were apparent.

Half awake, he serenely watched the sun slowly emerging from the Pacific Ocean. The vivid orange glowing orb sharply contrasted with the azure blue sea. He never tired of watching such a sunrise from this bed. He marveled at nature's splendor. The sun slowly cast its intense rays on the massive rocks of the picturesque El Arco, located to the east at the end of the beach where the crashing waves of the Pacific met the sedate blue water of the Sea of Cortez.

His sleepy gaze at these mesmerizing sights from his cliff top home in the Pedregal area of Cabo San Lucas was interrupted by another rising object. He turned to his left; gazing directly into the hazel brown, oval shaped eyes of a dark complexioned petite face sporting a mischievous smile. Her deep brown hair was cut like a picture frame designed to feature the beauty of her small perfect face. She gave him an impish look. She had just placed her small active hands under the black silk bed sheet, she was slowly softly massaging Garcia's most dominant body part. She worked her magic. He was up before the sun had fully risen.

With practiced precision, Carla accomplished her task and was quickly on top of Garcia's muscular six foot four inch frame. Her every move was planned, intense, powerful, and aggressive. Garcia lay back with a boyish grin and enjoyed his morning rise and shine wake-up call. The skills that he was enjoying were just one of the many talents of his chief administrative assistant. Besides being strikingly beautiful, she was extremely intelligent, with a Stanford MBA.

She both mystified and tantalized him whenever she was near. She could be a precise business person with insightful vision and impeccable grammar at one moment and a tempting dirty mouth slut in another second. He knew sex to her was either about satisfying herself or achieving her business objective. He often conjectured that she may have been a male in a prior life.

When Carla had mechanically finished with Garcia's wake-up call, she gave him a brief perfunctory kiss on the forehead. Without a word she walked slowly to the oversized bathroom. It's walls were covered with sheets of native Mexican black granite that had topaz strips and gold spots sprinkled intermittently throughout. The granite's colors fit perfectly with the thick forest green carpet and gold accessories. Each plush towel featured a large KG embossed in gold. The black bath tub was a made for two and could hold an NBA basketball team. A 65 inch plasma TV hung at the west end. The entire south side was a collapsible glass door that now stood entirely open.

She moved like a hunting tigress with gliding steps and a very feminine movement of her hips. As she waited for the shower to warm, she stretched her small muscular arms wide, sucking in deep breaths of the sea-scented air while looking out the open windows. The sun glistened on her naked body like stage spot lights.

Garcia sat on the edge of the bed and admired her small but strong frame as she continued her morning stretching and yoga positions in the rays of the morning sun. Her bronzed shoulders and back muscles were ripping and well defined from endless hours of weight work. The legs of her five foot four inch body were sinewy from miles of running followed by stretching exercises under the watchful eyes of her personal trainer. She was a goddess. But Garcia never doubted that he needed her more for her brains and cunning than sex.

Garcia, on one of his brief stops between jet set parties, had first met Carla when she was the chief personal assistant to his father, Hans Garcia; in another era known as U-boat Captain Hans Schier of Cologne, Germany. Hans had discovered Carla working as a computer consultant at a German CPA firm where she was on the fast track for partnership. She specialized in closings of international transactions. Hans hired her at double her salary and moved her to his business headquarters in Mexico City. There he meticulously educated her in all aspects of his legitimate interest, and insisted that she become fluent in English and Spanish as well as her native German language.

She worked wonders with modernizing the numerous legal Garcia ventures. New fuel efficient engines saved money in the cargo fleet, tankers and coastal runners. Upscale boats with bars and scantily clad waitresses enhanced revenues in the tourists fishing fleets. Improving the price, quality and variety of the trinkets sold by the vendors on all Mexican tourist beaches controlled by the Garcia Enterprises increased sales. Internet marketing and local financing tripled the timeshare revenues. Buying back programs for older but well-located timeshares locations followed by rehabbing and reselling them provided an instant jump start to a tired portion of the business.

Hans recognized her talents in negotiations and use of sex as a bargaining device when he sent her to acquire one aging competitor's properties located on the timeshare laden beaches at Cancun. Not only did she acquire the real estate for one-third less than he had allotted, she acquired a personal villa located in Cabo San Lucas high on the Pedregal cliffs overlooking the Pacific Ocean.

After selling these properties, Jose Mohado repeatedly called Hans, asking dumb financial questions. He always concluded that he needed Carla to come help him sort out the transaction. Carla relented once and thereafter refused to visit Jose. Her response was always the same, "Let the old goat go away. I got what I wanted, and so did he."

Hans quickly moved her compensation to a profit-sharing arrangement and introduced her to the illegal portions of the business. She attacked the goal of increasing profits from the illegal portions of Garcia Enterprises with the same skills, cunning, and endless energy.

New illegal ventures were initiated. Local factories were purchased to produce furniture with numerous hidden drawers and hollow legs designed to carry contraband to the U.S. Outlets for the furniture, minus the contraband, were established in numerous cities. Back hauls of used agricultural equipment and high end cars containing hidden weaponry from various Third World manufacturers were established. Used car lots in the U.S. were acquired to provide endless source of vehicles for use in the various smuggling operations across the U.S. borders. The rate of exporting illegal immigrants to the U.S. increased and the fee doubled.

Old illegal ventures were modernized. A bottling plant for manufacturing knock-off bottles of high priced alcohol was created to eliminate buying from other sources. Vodka, rum, and gin drinkers worldwide marveled at the low prices they paid for their top grade adult beverage from mass outlets located in large U.S. cities. It looked the same and tasted the same, but it was counterfeit. They never tried to match the taste of tequila, bourbon, or scotch as true consumers could tell the difference. They left that area to friends in Canada.

The distilling operations in the jungles outside of Mexico City were modernized and capacity tripled. Chemists repeatedly checked the quality and protocols. In addition, the small production and bottling plants were hidden in newly acquired residential homes concealed from the few honest authorities in the area.

The pot fields near the Texas borders were fertilized and new harvesting and drying techniques introduced. They were hidden by placing the product between rows of maze. The fields simply looked like very weedy corn patches.

The prostitution business was moved to upscale locations. Doctors were placed on retainers and party planners engaged. The number of high end orgies increased every time a new sexy party planner was hired. Both genders were well cared for by the planners. No taste was slighted. The old unsafe brothels were abandoned.

Hans was amazed at her creativity. She installed numerous accounting system improvements in order to analyze each proposed change. She was a constant source of fresh ideas on how to use their financial power and political influence for greater profit. More and more border guards and judges were placed on retainer. Political candidates were courted and acquired.

Hans, however, did rein her in on the desire to enter the meth business in the U.S. on a large scale. He had always avoided the opium and cocaine business leaving it to his friends. This also provided peace between the Mexican Mafia families. He refused to get into the meth business as he detested mind damaging drugs and refused to sell them or use them.

Even after Hans allowed her to seduce him several times in his office, he resisted her plans to move to the meth business. Despite her pouting and withdrawal of sex, he prevailed. She was a beauty and wonderful aphrodisiac for his aging sex life, but he knew sex was just a tool for Carla. He constantly warned his son to never use drugs, and never believe that you were seduced for love.

When Hans and his wife were assassinated within a few days of each other, Carla's new project was the control and influence of the sole heir to Garcia Enterprises. While son Kurt had the German genes of his father, Carla knew he did not have his brains or ambition. He hid his dyslexia very well. It was a clear limitation and frustration.

CHAPTER TWENTY-ONE

"A Smart Girl Is One Who Plays Tennis, Piano And Dumb."

LYNN REDGRAVE

*****

AFTER LEAVING Carla in the shower, Garcia enjoyed an hour of strenuous exercises and a deep muscle massage. Following this normal routine, he dressed slowly with a mind full of questions about the day's events.

He emerged into the large open breakfast area of the villa at a brisk pace. The large open eating area was filled with well kept lush tropical plants and flowers. A breeze from the sea moving through the open balcony area was refreshing. Wearing a white shirt, olive pants and a dark blue blazer, he looked like Errol Flynn, Clark Gable, or Rich Gere entering a movie set. He was strikingly handsome. Liv Garcia knew this was Garcia's business attire for a monthly meeting with his chief aids.

"You look delicious. I assume you have a long day ahead?"

"I do. Nice of you to ask. Where are your boys?"

"They are off to school. I have instructed two of your guards to stay very close to them. That last kidnap scare was too much for me to live through again. This brings up a subject I want to again discuss."

"I know this is another attempt on your part to revisit our deal. Liv, I have paid well over the last seven years for you and your boys to act like my wife and family. I know you have had several brushes with disaster, for which I am truly sorry. That last kidnapping attempt was a close call. You have to admit that the seven figures I pay you and being on my arm are not bad fringe benefits. In addition, I have never pushed you for sex. It's an option, not an obligation." He winked at her and gave his best boyish grin.

"It's not about money, Kurt. It's about my fear that someday an attempt to get at you will cost my boys and me dearly. You have always been fair and a charming companion. The occasional romance has also been very pleasant, but I want to leave while my boys and I are alive. Let's figure out a way for me to disappear with them back to Sweden and be done with this life as your make believe wife and family."

Garcia slowly sipped on his dark brown coffee and nibbled a few berries as he thought about her words. He knew he needed to talk to Carla on the logistics of moving Liv out of his life. He knew what needed to be done. He rather enjoyed the thought of being alone again.

"Give me one more performance and I will work it out. I likely will need you to act as security while I negotiate a new and very important deal in the U.S. You and the boys will be safe and get a chance to visit a new area called Iowa."

With narrowing eyes and an evil grin, he continued. "After that trip, I will work out a way for this life with me to end. I knew when I hired you after your modeling career imploded, thanks to your cocaine issues that this would never be a lifetime arrangement."

Liv hung her head as she knew her bout with cocaine had brought her and the boys to this life. A small tear dropped on her cheek as she again admitted that her weakness had put her two boys repeatedly at risk and likely caused the death of their father. She knew instinctively that the his death from an overdose a few weeks after she met Garcia was not an accident.

Garcia's proposed arrangement of Liv and her boys acting as his public family came shortly after the funeral. She accepted the offer, dried out with his doctor's help, and played her role to perfection. She had no choice. The money was great, and the children were educated in the best of private schools. She also feared his vicious side which was ever present and unpredictable.

"Thank you Kurt. I will play one more role. When that job is done, I would like a new face, new visas, credit cards, and other travel papers. I intend to return to Farth, the small town in Sweden where the boys can grow up without the fear of being blown up or diced up by your enemies."

Garcia slowly sipped his coffee. "You have been loyal, so it's agreed to. I just need to figure out a plausible way to make it happen."

He knew he lied, but it bought him time to talk to Carla. He looked at his watch.

"I need to leave for my pre-meeting briefing and then an all day meeting with my five business unit heads. Why don't you take one of the jets and run over to Mexico City for a little shopping?"

He knew she would go, shop briefly, and find herself in bed with one of his shipping customers, Ricardo Blanco. He didn't care. It kept Blanco as a loyal client. It would later serve as a way to extort money from him. She had served her purpose.

CHAPTER TWENTY-TWO

"An Accountant Is Someone Who Solves A Problem You Didn't Know You Had In A Way You Don't Understand."

K ATHERINE W HITETHORN

✶✶✶✶✶

AS GARCIA ENTERED his bedroom, he noticed that the 10x10 glass table affixed on a massive black granite rock was filled with stacks of paper for this meeting with Carla. He cringed as he saw the four-inch stack resting in front of his chair. Carla had already completed her review and was waiting for his executive briefing. She was attired in a black suit which was tightly tailored to display her petite but strong body. Her purple silk blouse was deep cut to display two of her best negotiating tools.

Carla knew to keep it simple. Garcia had never worked at developing his mind. He was likely dyslexic, but clearly had been mentally lazy his entire early life. He had enjoyed the role of the family party animal and stud never thinking that someday he would need to step into his father's shoes. His only redeeming intellectual characteristic was that he listened carefully to her and could fake enough general observations to appear thoughtful and smart. Carla knew to be careful not to insult him. He had a vicious side that could erupt and knew no limits.

"The five business unit managers only care about their profits and safety, but you need them. They are all your father's old friends. Their German ambition and attention to detail cannot be replaced. They know each business group's activities in unbelievable detail. They are loyal to his name and afraid of you. Your elimination of the Aveigia family because of their involvement in your father's death left a deep impression."

With a long gaze checking Garcia's comprehension, followed by a charming smile Carla continued to lecture.

"I want you to look at each of them without blinking and ask why profits are slipping. Give them each a chance to talk. Ask open-ended questions that will cause them talk more about their business. For example, 'Very interesting. Can you explain that for me? I like where you are going, but can you help me understand how you will get there? I think I understand but can you be more specific? And the old stand-by, I don't think I follow, can you clarify your thought?' Asking good questions always makes you look smarter and well prepared"

Carla snickered. "Executives worldwide have been using these open ended questions, between deep thoughtful looks and pauses for years as a substitute for in-depth understanding."

She flinched as Garcia did not laugh. She had gone too far.

With a long, deep glare he coldly said, "What else do I need to say, my ingenious resourceful assistant?"

"After the initial review ask them to bring back their thoughts for the next meeting. Tell them about your love and trust of them and how you cherish their undoubting loyalty to you and the memory of your father. That bunch of BS will disarm them. We need to get this next deal done before we replace them. They are old and out of touch."

He nodded. "When do we introduce the Iowa meth deal?"

"After dinner, before you bring in the new batch of whores I hired, pour them some expensive Port and turn to me. I will give them a quick review. They will be too drunk and horny to object with any real effort."

The meeting started at lunch. All five business unit managers were dressed in the latest European pants, shirts, and blazers. Each was one of his father's loyal German officers who had migrated from Cologne to Mexico late in 1944 with Captain Hans Schier aboard U-3334. The money Hans had stolen from the Third Reich before its collapse had served all of them very well over the years.

Everything proceeded as Carla had predicted, except for the action of Bertram Schroeder. After a lavish dinner of old country delicacies, Carla, with charts and Power Points, reviewed their small profits from pot sales in the US.

"We are selling pot in small U.S. towns on a steady basis. Those depressed rural areas are perfect targets. However, the local pot growers are holding down our market penetration. These small town people are afraid of our Mexican sellers and the products sold by the local growers are very cheap. The best solution is not to have a turf war with the locals but to merge with them. We can use their pot marketing, and introduce meth on a large scale, before we eliminate their leaders."

She struck a very sexy pose, her breast bursting at their seams, as she leaned forward and looked at each of them. Everyone was nodding except for Bertram.

She began, "We have unlimited amounts of Pseudoephedrine from our Asian sources. The potheads in the rural areas can acquire anhydrous ammonia by buying it as fertilizer from local farm cooperatives. We will make it right there in rural America. This proximity of manufacturing cuts down time of shipping the finished product reduces risk of loss and dramatically cuts expenses. It will produce at least a billion per year. It does not conflict with the Torres family's cocaine or opium business."

She knew the greed factor was taking control.

"I have our first merger located. It is in small town Iowa. A local pot grower has ingeniously developed an underground drying and bagging system. It is in a cave network under a large hill, impossible to detect. He has bribed local farmers into planting obscure valleys full of pot so his source is convenient and cheap. He set up his sales system like a pyramid business such as Tupperware. His market controls most of Iowa, Missouri, and Nebraska. If we had his business, we could quickly enlarge his underground production facility and add meth and expand his sales force."

Bertram finally broke his silence. "I know from a business prospective you are right. I simply have a hard time breaking from Han's long and unwavering refusal to get into heavy mind-damaging drugs. I likely will vote against it."

After a few silent stares passed and the sound of silence grew, Garcia put his hand on Bertram shoulder. "Old friend, let's all spend the night thinking about the idea and reconvene tomorrow at breakfast. I have 10 Cabo's best little brown love machines for you. Each of them is beautiful, charming and in need of your attention."

The meeting ended abruptly. All 10 LBLMs were dark-haired, black-eyed, well toned, adorned with jewelry, and clad in very shear negligees. The old men, like men world over, stopped and began to think with their small but dominant alternative brain.

CHAPTER TWENTY-THREE

"No Good Decision Was Ever Made In A Swivel Chair."

GEORGE S. PATTON JR.

★★★★★

TWO WEEKS AFTER Bertram Schroeder's funeral, Garcia flew to Iowa to meet with Jesse Marvin to start the merger process. Garcia was amazed with Bertram's fortuitous demise from a heart attack. He was always vigorous in his workout habits, weight, and eating habits. The good news was he was gone as he alone had blocked this merger. Garcia returned from his visit in a euphoric mood.

On the balcony of his villa he watched another sunset and consumed several shots of tequila. Carla listened intently as he rambled about his brilliant negotiating skills. She never flinched, smirked, or smiled. He can learn some elementary things, she thought silently.

"The trip was a success. Marvin is very cautious, but very greedy. He quickly understood why we can be a profitable fit. I sense he is very easy to underestimate. He is small, unshaven, disheveled, and speaks terrible English. He acts like a real hillbilly. He has an irritating habit of constantly licking his upper lip when he is thinking. When that habit is combined with his green eyes, it's easy to see why he is nicknamed The Lizard."

Garcia took out a map and pointed first to Iowa then to Pisgah. "The area where he operates is located in an extremely rural area. It lies in a massive chain of small mountains called the Loess Hills. The police authorities' manpower is limited, so he operates freely. He has spies everywhere as he spreads money around very efficiently. He knows how to operate in an undetectable fashion. Once we have his business and system, he means nothing to us."

Garcia finally understand the potential that Carla had projected from the merger. Marvin's underground cave production site was brilliantly conceived and nearly undetectable. The logistics for moving product over the background of rural mid-America was nearly foolproof. The market was obvious. As the small towns of America decayed, their citizens cried for an easy fix to briefly enjoy life again.

Only Carla knew the truth about Bertram's recent deadly heart attack in bed with one of her best brown love machines. A quick shot of potassium-chloride had accelerated his aging heart beyond its capacity. His death preceded the vote on the Midwest meth project. Now support for this project was unanimous and enthusiastic. The project was totally in Garcia's hands to develop. In reality it was in Carla's control.

As Carla predicted, a week later Marvin arrived at the Cabo villa on one of Garcia's Lear jets. Garcia was well coached. He charmed the wily, scruffy little man from Pisgah. Despite his appearance, Garcia and Carla were impressed by Marvin's caution and survival skills. His two huge Bosnian body guards were ever present and appeared dangerous and unwaveringly loyal. The small man's blazing green eyes and reptilian-like tongue constantly moistening his lip were disconcerting. His backwoods language and manners were deceptive.

Garcia had enticed Marvin and his guards to leave Iowa and come to Cabo to discuss business by offering his beloved wife Liv and two children as security. Marvin felt secure as long as they stayed in Iowa visiting the state's many historical sites and roaming in the Loess Hills surrounding Jesse's underground production facility. Garcia's love for his family was obvious to Marvin. He was very wrong.

In Cabo, Carla led the meetings and laid out the merger idea and all its merits. She accurately predicted Jesse's initial rejection of the idea. She also predicted that a few million dollars upfront payment, after a few nights with her lovely female LBLMs, would overcome the resistance. She did not tell Garcia that she personally consummated the deal two nights before. A night with Carla convinced Marvin that the new partnership would be profitable and exciting as his little brain took total control of his survival instincts. Besides the money, the fringe benefits of working with Carla were very enticing.

Men worldwide have succumbed to such persuasive tactics exclusively controlled by the female gender. Similar tactics by men always tend to fail and are labeled sexual harassment.

After four days of discussions, planning, and partying, Marvin went home. He carried with him five camouflage backpacks stuffed with over two million dollars. Unknown to him the money bands and bags also contained tracking devices inserted by Carla. The Lizard's deep tongued kiss and buttock squeeze as he boarded the plane left Carla cringing. She smiled and gave a slight moan of pleasure.

After the terms of merger were agreed upon, Carla attacked the process and details with relentless energy. She executed the merger plans with flawless precision. She quickly dispatched engineers and workers to substantially enlarge and reinforce Marvin's underground cave and install the mixing and drying equipment for the meth. The new manpower quietly moved into the very rural Iowa area. In order to avoid detection they lived in various adjacent small towns, drove old vehicles, and used the hidden north entrance to the cave complex to avoid detection of their work and soil removal.

The local contractors who had first built the cave, the Sharpe brothers, were soon dispensable. Their knowledge was absorbed by the new crew and their pot addiction had been converted to meth addiction. They died in a convenient cave-in early in the expansion.

Carla was tireless in holding meetings with Marvin's sales force. She was especially adept at winning the loyalty of the sales leaders. Her flirtatious demeanor left each sales leader convinced he would get screwed by her. They were right on the result, not the technique. In a matter of a few months Carla knew all of the sales force, had converted them to selling meth, and had assumed all necessary communications. The local sales leaders were usually too stoned to stay engaged. The Lizard's brother, Henry, had expanded the clever sales system and staffed it with good old boy hillbillies. They were all dispensable.

Carla also quickly dominated the key sources of the necessary anhydrous ammonia. The small-time, nearly bankrupt, hill farmers were crushed when they first found their pot growing business income would be seriously reduced. They were then delighted when Carla explained how she would buy their expensive liquid fertilizer with her money. This payoff was for merely ordering one-third more fertilizer than they needed and looking the other way when the excess was removed.

Their allegiance to Carla was further enhanced when, as a reward for being so cooperative, Carla arranged for a special trip to Omaha. A night at Minnie's Bar and Grill enjoying a great steak, too much liquor, and an evening in Minnie's bed was the high point of their year, maybe their life. The secretly taken graphic pictures of their pathetic actions with Minnie's daughter were also very influential in assuring their loyalty to Carla.

Marvin, to Carla's surprise, was extremely cooperative. Carla made sure he received his money on time and made sure he took a few trips back to Cabo for a visit with the LBLMs. Despite her dislike for him, she occasionally had sex with him to elicit necessary information. Carla found the sex disgusting, but her need to control the merger integration process dominated her actions.

The Lizard's smirk while they had sex left her extremely uncomfortable. He may be using her while she was using him. She accepted the sacrifice knowing his time was limited. He was nearly unnecessary to the going forward process. The integration was proceeding like her MBA thesis on efficient integration techniques.

CHAPTER TWENTY-FOUR

"Mexico: Where Life Is Cheap, Death Is Rich And The Buzzards Are Never Unhappy."

EDWARD ABBEY

✷✷✷✷✷

GARCIA FELT THE Sun glowing on his face as it rose from the Pacific Ocean's horizon. He slowly began to wake and rolled over to his left. Carla's side of the bed was unslept in again. Carla had been ignoring him for weeks. She obsessed with every detail of building the new Iowa site and the transition. He walked into her office and found her fully clothed asleep on the couch. He tried softly massaging her back, buns and calves, hoping to arouse her for a little wake up sex.

Her brown beautiful eyes popped open. A flash of anger at being aroused was quickly harnessed. She gave him a kiss on the cheek and called the servants for coffee.

"Tomorrow we are off to Iowa for the Grand Opening. Everything is running on time. If this merger works like I have planned, we can supply the entire Midwest. Then we can set up similar operations throughout each of the rural areas of the United States. It is also at last my time to say good-bye to that rotten, dirty little Lizard."

He pouted as he watched her shower. She was beautiful. He knew she was motivated by the billion dollar venture. Sex with him was not necessary or even interesting today. After a long sip of coffee, Garcia looked at Carla.

"I am not going to be there. I am sending one of my stand-ins. I need to fulfill my promise and let Liv and her boys leave this life. I think being a sorrowful widower suits me. Don't you?"

"I will also send my cousin Martin to help with the celebration in Iowa." Carla nodded her approval.

"Tell me, Carla, how will the Lizard meet his fate?"

Her eyes were dancing. A grin filled her face. "He has an office at the west end of the cave where he works and lives. He and his girl-friend will be killed when a small unexplained explosion occurs during the celebrations. His brother who runs the sales force is always by his side as are the two big Bosnian guards. In one small cave-in, the merger power transfer will be completed. Just like it happens in any textbook on merger transition planning."

Garcia sipped his deep brown coffee, smiled and nodded. Could anything be that simple, he thought? Carla picked up her briefcase and a small bag, then gave him a cheek kiss.

"Enjoy your trip with Liv," she said with a wink and an impish grin.

THE USUAL limousine did not pick up Liv, the boys, and Garcia. A smaller Lincoln Navigator appeared. A new driver introduced himself as Vincent. When they all were in the car it proceeded north to the San Jose Cabo Airport. Liv was beautiful. Her blue Nordic eyes were alive and happy. She was chattering endlessly. She was excited about her new-found freedom.

"You have been a wonderful companion over the years. Maybe after awhile you can come to Sweden and meet me. We can start this relationship on a normal basis?"

"I agree, but for now we need a break, Liv. People cannot figure out you and the boys have disappeared, or you won't remain safe for long. Here is my plan. After I put you on my jet for Sweden, this car will be headed back to the villa, it will explode and plunge into the sea. The news will report your tragic end. I will survive, as I stayed here and took a cab to another meeting. You have enough money for a face-lift and two years living expenses. I will find you when I feel it's safe."

"It sounds so simple. Will it work?"

Just like Carla planned, he thought. "Don't worry. All steps are arranged to perfection."

At the private terminal where Garcia's Lear Jets were stored, Garcia stepped out and gave Liv and the boys a brief kiss. As he walked into the terminal, the limo rolled on the tarmac towards the waiting jet. He hit the detonator button once, twice, three times. The car erupted in a ball of fire and flying metal.

Garcia ran into the terminal, faked a few sobs, and cried for a call to the police.

Everyone jumped out of their trance at seeing the car smoldering on the tarmac. "Tell Chief Roberto that the Torres family has killed my family."

Garcia was pleased with his thespian efforts. He followed Carla's script to the letter, wishing the process would hurry up. He wanted to go back to the villa and turn on the 28 surveillance cameras Carla had installed and focused on all parts of the cave complex. He wanted to watch the celebrations in Iowa and cheer when The Lizard became a pile of smoldering compost.

Garcia dialed his cell phone. "Carla, have you landed? Is everything going as planned?"

The female voice was soft, quick, and unfamiliar. "We are nearly there Mr. Garcia."

CHAPTER TWENTY-FIVE

*"I Had An Interest In Death From An Early Age. It Fascinated
Me. When I Heard Humpty Dumpty Sat On The Wall, I Thought,
Did He Fall Or Was He Pushed? "*

P.D. JAMES

*****

CARLA, MARTIN, and Ernesto, the Garcia look-alike, arrived in
Omaha on the Lear 55 at 10 a.m. The Loess Hill bluffs overlooking
the Omaha Epply Field Airport to the east were springing alive with
new vegetation. The tree covered slopes of the bluffs were like an Irish
mural with vivid and varied shades of dark green trees, bushes and prairie grasses.

VALLI HAD BEEN warned of their arrival the night before when
Snyder's FFA bug warned of a Lear jet filing a flight plan from Cabo
to Omaha. He made the two hour drive to Epply Field and, dressed as
a lawn care employee, watched them as they got off the plane. He was
awestruck at the beauty of the woman and size of the men. He hopped
into an old rusty Dodge pickup and followed them out of the airport. He
knew their destination, so he could afford to keep a safe distance behind

them. He turned on his computer and watched the activity at the cave. The bird's eye camera showed many people scurrying around the cave.

Fielding called and reported that his listening rocks were picking up many references to Garcia and a fiesta.

Valli took a side road and entered Pisgah from the south avoiding the route through Little Sioux which was the direct and normal route to the cave. With his computer and the bird's camera, he had a perfect view of the process from five miles away on a side road north of Pisgah headed to Moorhead. He tested the triggering device. It was engaged. One call would launch the rocket. The merger would go up in a pile of dust. He knew this was it. He was done and retired. He would not take this risk again.

THE ONE HOUR RIDE on I-29 to the Little Sioux exit to Pisgah was uneventful. They all could see the grass and bush covered dome housing Jesse's cave from miles away as they knew its exact location. The casual observer would never notice it as it appeared like just another tall mound rising from a Loess Hill. Carla and Martin rehearsed their plan. Just before the operation was to be started up for the first time by the technicians and the celebration initiated, they would send Marvin with his group to his portion of the cave for more wine and food. The explosive in that area had already been planted.

The newly arrived visitors to the cave were amply impressed. Under the dome of a large round hill atop one of the highest Loess Hills over-looking the Missouri River Valley laid four acres of warehousing and production. The 20 foot high ceiling was supported by massive multi-colored I-beams. The heating and cooling ducts ran in all directions barely below the roofline giving the appearance of octopus tentacles. The concrete floor was perfect in texture and smoothness. Lighting dispersed from the ceiling left no shadows.

The east one-third portion contained the mixing, drying, and pack-aging operations. Because of the potential of an explosion from the process involving the stored anhydrous ammonia, it was sealed off from the rest by a one-foot thick fireproof wall. Next to that wall stood the delivery fleet; thirty rusting nondescript cars with perfect motors, tires, and transmissions. A state of the art repair station stood silently by them ready to immediately provide any repairs. The rest of the area contained racks for storage of meth and drying, cutting, and storage of pot.

At the far west end of the complex was another walled off portion containing Jesse's living area. It was filled with computers, observation equipment, video games, electric gadgets and two pounds of explosive placed under his bed by Carla.

The celebration was conducted perfectly. The meth cooking was starting. Scientists smiled as their equipment began to mix, gurgle, and bubble. The specially invited sales force smiled at the prospects of making millions. Their twitching and sniffing actions clearly indicated they had sampled as much marketing product as they had distributed. Carla's plan was to eliminate them over two months and replace them with her people.

"Jesse, your cooperation has made this perfect. I hope the fringe benefits I have provided on our marketing trips can continue." Carla purred.

"Carla, no more bullshit. I know you won't need me anymore. I likely will move up north to my cousin's at Fargo. I want to hunt, fish, and enjoy my profits. By the way, I enjoyed being used by you," Jesse softly whispered as he licked his upper lip.

Carla smiled and nodded. She put a hand on his shoulder.

"Be a dear and go get a couple of cases of wine, beer, and other booze that we stored in your room. Bring the gifts I had delivered as a reward for the technician's hard work."

She jumped from her golf cart and said, "Use my golf cart to haul it over to this area. Would you also round up Stella, your brother, and the two Bosnian mastodons and have them help you, and then join us? I have a gift for them. If you are fast, I will. as my personal gift to you, use you one more time for old time's sake, Mr. Lizard."

Jesse smiled and departed on the golf cart licking his smiling lips. As he looked back and waved, Carla briefly thought. "He looks too happy."

Carla returned to the mixing area, toasted the crew and hugged each visitor. The technicians were pouring the meth ingredients into the mixing tanks and were heating up the cooking process. Everyone was laughing and slapping each other's back. The system worked perfectly. Suddenly, Carla froze in stark terror as one of the anhydrous ammonia tanks exploded. The fire set off repeated explosions of the other tanks. She instantly dove to the floor and heard a larger explosion from the far west end of the cave. She knew The Lizard was no more.

The next fraction of a second passed like life was frozen in place. Other huge explosions rocked the complex, and the entire roof came tumbling down on her and everyone in the area. She never had time to scream as tons of steel and Loess dirt crushed her.

The explosion at the west end of the complex sent Jesse flying out the exit door rolling down the slope. He had luckily survived the blast. When it occurred, he had stepped out of the cave to breathe the pure clear air one last time before running away to a safer place. Stella, his only love, had left unnoticed two days earlier with the two loyal body guards.

Jesse had known his days were limited and an early fatal retirement was imminent. With plenty of cash, new identifications, and a plastic surgeon's name, he was on his way for a rendezvous in Minneapolis. He had committed to Stella to disappear, get a new identity, and find an honest life free of guilt from meth burning up users' minds and fear of a quick death from his partners.

Running like a deer through the woods to the north of the cave, he hoped he avoided detection from the surveillance cameras planted in the tree line by keeping his green John Deere hat pulled low. As he leapt into his rusting Chevy pickup hidden in the bramble bushes at the base of the hill, he glanced up. He was overwhelmed with the sight of the enormous cave complex imploding and disappearing into a cloud of brown Loess Hill's dust.

He was confused. He knew his room had exploded, and his small charge in the mixing room went off. The other explosions were hard to comprehend. He knew he had eliminated most of the Garcia leaders, but he had seen the gray eyes of the Garcia look-alike. Garcia's eyes were deep brown. Garcia was alive. He also thought, but he was not sure, he felt a difference when he patted Carla's butt and gave her boobs a farewell squeeze. It wasn't her. They would be seeking revenge.

VALLI SAT IN HIS PICKUP in total confusion. He had been ready to push the triggering device when everyone was well-situated in the cave. Then he saw a puff of smoke and dust from the east end of the cave followed by another from the west end. Neither explosion seemed to be large enough to destroy the cave. He hit the fire button and the rocket added to the mayhem.

As he watched the implosion, he saw a figure rolling down the hill from the west end. Someone had survived. He called Snyder to see if he could get on line with the bird's eye cameras and get a picture of the witness.

As he headed back to Des Moines, Snyder's call came.

"Good news and bad news. We got a facial picture as the guy hopped into his pickup. We cannot identify him, but he is little and wearing a dirty John Deere hat. It looks to me like some of the previous pictures we have of the same guy with the two big bodyguards and the little skinny girl. My bet is that Jesse Marvin is the sole survivor."

CHAPTER TWENTY-SIX

"Never Under Estimate A Man Who Over Estimates Himself."

FRANKLIN D. ROOSEVELT

*****

GARCIA SAT FROZEN in his office chair. His eyes danced. Sweat gushed down his forehead. His eyes were red as dying coals. He watched and re-watched the tape showing the Iowa disaster unravel. He watched his team entering the complex with smiles on their faces. It sent shivers up his spine. He thought of their last minutes, choking to death in a heap of Loess Hill dirt.

The small puff of smoke at the east end might have been an explosion. The bigger puff of smoke at the west end, housing Marvin's area, was obviously part of Carla's plan. The puzzling event was the following next destructive explosions and resulting imploding of the complex. The mystery of the multiple explosions maddened him. His only explanation was The Lizard had tried to get his team before they got him. Could he have been that shrewd?

One thing was clear; one small person had escaped. The green hat pulled down to eye level, as that person ran through the forest trail was a telltale clue. The person's identity was confirmed from a brief security camera picture of Jesse's smirking face looking back at the catastrophe.

He was just entering a rusty old pickup. Garcia's anger escalated each time he reviewed the picture.

His anger was reaching a nearly out of control state. He was frustrated, doubting he could recreate this billion dollar opportunity without Carla. His dyslexic mind deterred his understanding of Carla's numerous and extensive plans for creating and operating this plant and its marketing system. He was crazed. He could not understand Carla's notes describing a method for tracking Jesse's activity if he should ever disappear.

Garcia's paranoia was building. His empire was badly damaged by these events, and he could not interpret the numbers and reports that flooded his desk. He quickly withdrew from everyone, became reclusive, and doubled his guards at the Cabo villa.

He was very alone. His irrational mind reasoned that his four remaining advisors had lost confidence and wanted the empire for themselves.

Carla was buried somewhere below the rubble in Pisgah, Iowa. Her brains and cunning would be impossible to replace. He knew how dependent he was on her. He realized how little he could trust his father's old friends and business associates. They had no respect for him. They were just another enemy. They must be dealt with.

For two weeks he had been violating his father's golden rule: Never sample your own product. He had never tried meth before, but in a desperate need for relief from the building frustrations, he tried a sample. For two weeks he had been on repeated ever-escalating meth highs. His mood swings were from manic to depressed and then to paranoid. He seldom ate. He never bathed. He chased his servants away with a loaded Uzi. Every downer and mood swing caused him to escalate the usage.

In one of his manic trips, he knew he was at risk as the competitors could sense weakness. He had only one answer. He had to kill them. While he was killing them, why not eliminate his father's old friends? Then he would somehow find and kill The Lizard.

The first two steps of his plan would be easy and maybe even enjoyable. Garcia was doing what he did best, using violence. Killing a few old business friends meant nothing to him. The challenges of locating Marvin, however, were swirling in his already stressed mind. He had Carla's scribbled notes about tracking devices. He was too confused and disoriented to understand them.

He had not slept in days. Every time he tried sleep, he saw green eyed lizards all around him. Their tongues were licking their lips. When he looked out of his bedroom window, the beautiful sunset over the Pedregal's bluffs meant nothing. The beach below was covered with thousands of green eyed lizards looking up at his home. Their tongues were flicking in rhythm.

He knew he had to find and kill Marvin before the lizards on the beach, which were endlessly emerging from the sea, consumed him. With that brilliant thought, he took one more pull on his fifth pipe of meth for the day and fell back into his bed. His ravished mind gradually drifted back to better days. His gaunt, dirty face smiled as he slipped into contented dreams of waking to view the sunrise and feeling Carla's hands reach for him.

He floated like a cloud looking down at a once handsome man collapsed in a chair; glowing pipe in one hand and a gold plated police model .38 S&W Colt in the other. The rumpled hair, hollow unshaven cheeks, and the glowing red eyeballs appeared to him as a demon growing in place of the human. Suddenly, the exhaustion, resulting from the meth let-down, hit his brain. He spiraled into a fitful spinning blackness like so many of his customers thanks to the magic of meth. All he saw were dark shadows with an occasional green eyed lizard gazing at him as it licked its upper lip. The Colt in his shaking right hand slowly moved upward.

FROM AN ADJACENT DOORWAY, Vaughn Mueller, the oldest of the surviving Garcia business managers leaned over and softly spoke, "Carla dear, it's time. Do we let him do it or save him for our use as an intimidator while we recover what is left of this business? He can be helpful in finding and eliminating that hillbilly who outsmarted us. His brain is nearly fried, and he is quite confused. I think we can control him as long as we need him to transition the business to us. He will really go off into total swirling confusion when he recognizes that you are alive. Too bad poor Neita had to die in that cave in. She was so beautiful, your perfect clone. You had good instincts in sending her to the celebration when you knew Kurt was sending his clone. It saved you."

Vaughn gave the lecherous smile of a seventy-five year old. "You and Neita even made love alike. What a waste. Well, you now have what you wanted, control of Garcia Enterprise. Use him as you want."

Justice And Revenge For A Price

****

PART FOUR

"Your Most Dangerous Competitors Are Those
That Are Most Like You."

B ARBARA F OLLET

CHAPTER TWENTY-SEVEN

" Never Trust Anyone Who Wants What You've Got. Friend Or No, Envy Is An Overwhelming Emotion. "

E U B I E   B L A K E

✱✱✱✱✱

JESSE FELT suspended in mid-air. Seconds before, he was standing in the west door of the cave complex getting a last deep breath of clean hill air when the first explosion occurred. The explosion at the east end was no surprise as he had set it and had just hit the detonator. The explosion at the west end where he lived took him by surprise and launched him into space. He thought he heard another explosion as he hit the ground. He rolled and glanced back. As he came to earth, he saw the complex rise in the air and then sink into a four acre crater. He ran with all his might.

He knew Garcia was alive, and was confident Carla was alive. His parting squeeze of her boobs and butt felt different; less firm. Contrary to most male's mentality, they do not all feel the same. He knew he was a marked man, as was everyone around him.

He jumped into his rusted pickup and drove through the wandering back roads as fast as he had ever gone. A cloud of dust rose behind him. His teeth chattered as he flew over the rough rutted roads. The seven foot tall pampas grass in the ditches flashed by so fast they appeared like a solid curtain. When he exited the hills, he drove directly west until he intersected old Highway 75. He shot north at 90 miles an hour on the aging broken up pavement until he hit Onawa and then took I-29 to the Sioux City International Airport. He started to breath regularly, instead of in gasps, when from over five miles away he could see the huge runway of the aging WWII B-17 training field.

He parked the pickup in an illegal parking zone, leaving the window down and the motor running. He tried to look calm as he jogged to the counter with a large aging duffle bag over his shoulder. Luckily, the only flight to Minneapolis was just an hour away. He paid for the ticket using his new credit card in the name of Rex Rice and checked the duffle bag like any other bag. The beat-up camouflage bag contained ten smaller Pioneer Seed logo covered bags with five million in cash in them. Unfortunately, these bags still had Carla's well placed tracing chips in the grip.

On landing, Jesse grabbed a cab and went directly to the Holiday Inn Express located directly off of I-94. He picked up a room key at the front desk as Mrs. Rex Rice had already arrived two days before. His new driver's license and credit cards again worked perfectly. Jesse Marvin had just disappeared.

He entered the large State Room and looked at the body lying in the bed. "Mrs. Rice, you look like you got hit by a freight train." He gingerly examined the surgical gauze covering most of Stella's face.

"Those chin straps looks like your head is tied together."

Tears welled in her eyes as she stood and opened her arms to hug him.

"What all did that plastic surgery guy do to you?"

Through swollen lips, She smiled. Big tears rolled from her deep brown eyes, across her purple puffed lids and down her swollen cheeks. "You are alive and safe. Give me a kiss and hug, but be careful. My face feels like a balloon that could explode."

He held her tight. He had never experienced the feeling of caring for someone and craving a simple touch from her.

"Honey you look great to me. What did you have done,? How do you feel? And when will you get better?"

"I had an eyebrow lift to open up my eyes, the shape of my eyes changed and permanent eye liner applied to accentuate my new beautiful eyes. My lower eyes had fat removed. My nose was straightened and shortened. My cheeks have implants inserted to make them rounder. My chin has an implant to make it appear stronger and the sagging skin below my chin was eliminated. My thin lips were injected so they are now pleasantly plump. Other than that, I am the same."

"Wow, are you in pain? I am about to get a new face tomorrow. Maybe there is time to back out."

"Actually, I just feel puffy. There is very little pain. He really is good. It pays to get a young plastics guy and get the latest technique. I told him I wanted to look different, not just a younger version of myself. He had a hard time with that concept, but got on board when I paid cash. He definitely avoided the Joan Rivers and Carol Burnett pull back technique."

"Jesse, I mean Rex, you are having your nose shortened, eye lids raised, a strong chin implant with a dimple, and some chiseled cheek implants. Your ears are going to get reduced and tucked tight to your head. You will no longer look like a car with both doors open. Your hair will be colored deep brown eliminating its dishwater blonde look. Your puffy upper lip will be reduced. In addition, your teeth will have veneer added to make them straight and cover the brown and yellow color from years of bad hygiene. No more tobacco chewing for you. You won't be a movie star, but you will be close."

They hugged. If it weren't for the drains from the oozing stitches, long passionate love making was in order. Instead they just held hands and smiled about their escape. The idea of a new life was a dream come true too both of them. Jesse could not bring himself to rain on a happy moment by discussing the fact that Garcia would soon be after them.

That night they fell asleep in a tight hug with legs and arms entwined. The next morning room service arrived. They had a breakfast of fruit, yogurt, whole grain toast, and oatmeal. Jesse eyed the display.

"Where are the fried eggs, bacon, hash browns, ketchup, and white toast?"

"Mr. Rice, you are changing your habits and becoming health conscious. I have been doing a lot of reading, and we have a lot of changing to do. Anyway, your old habits might tip someone off as to what a hillbilly you really are."

He dabbed at the oatmeal and covered the toast with butter. He nodded. "Will I be ready to travel in a week or less?"

"If you behave for a couple of days, I was told its okay to travel, but no lifting or exercising. It will take two to three weeks to get the swelling down. Why the time concern? We are new rich people."

"Stella, we need to keep moving and get up north to the safe house in Nisswa. We can contact Henry, Rufkin, and Otto once we have hunkered down in the lakes and woods of northern Minnesota. By the way, when can we screw?"

A solid punch to the shoulder followed as his answer.

She laughed. "Give me another tranquilizer and get yourself a bag to cover my head and have at it you horny hillbilly. After tonight I won't screw anyone as homely as you!"

"RUFKIN AND OTTO had never seen so much money. They kept the two bags under their bed, but periodically got it out to recount it and take a little fun money. They knew they had been repeatedly directed by Jesse to find a place in Minneapolis that was not high profile, not to spend money like they were rich, and wait for Jesse's call on their disposable cell phones. But they were like boys in a candy shop, an alcoholic in a liquor store or a fat girl in a bakery.

They were infatuated with the N.E. Art Galleries and Study district located along Central Avenue and N.E. Broadway. They rented a suite at the Four Points by Sheraton which was larger than anything they had every lived in. They shopped for new clothes, tried upscale expensive restaurants, and fell into the active night life. They loved the 331 Club, Dusty's and The Anchor. They found that picking up local female artists, was not all that hard. Their money bought them a great deal of charm.

For the first time in their lives they did not need to get up early. They fell into a pattern of sleeping late, working out, touring the area and chasing female artists all night. Using cabs became boring so they leased a black Escalade SUV. They felt it helped their lady pickup efforts. Unfortunately, it also made them noticed by the locals.

Ten days after their arrival, they were wandering back to The Four Point with a couple of cute starving artists in tow. The cool early fall night was starting to sober them up. Their minds were oblivious to any risk. The hands of the artists were actively groping their new found rich daddies. The tall, large boned, blue eyed blondes slide her hands into the front of Otto's pants.

"You are big all over aren't you my new friend? Erma will make you even bigger." She giggled. Otto gave a drunken grin and nodded.

Otto looked at his lifetime buddy who was suddenly leaning against the wall while the smaller blond blue eyed artist was pulling his smaller brain from his unzipped pants. Both men were giggling.

Suddenly, two large dark figures stepped from a car behind them. Both Rufkin and Otto froze in terror as the two probes from the stun guns hit them in the neck. They fell like rocks. The two young starving artists were two strides into a run when the bullets from the suppressed guns dropped them. They also fell like rocks. The shooters picked up the two unconscious men and roughly tossed them into the back of the SUV. Without losing a stride, they then put two more bullets into the head of each artist.

Rufkin felt like he was coming out of a fog. He was shaking his head trying to clear it. He was disoriented. He felt his hands duct taped tightly to a chair. His head was duct tapped to the back of the chair. He tried to puke but his mouth was covered. His eyes finally focused, and across from him was Otto's body. It was strapped to a chair just like him. Blood dripped from where his fingers used to be and his face was filled with deeply embedded nails. He did not move or show any sign of breathing.

Wild crazy fear shot through Rufkin's mind. He had seen death many times, he had seen torture, but the condition of Otto's lifeless body sent him into frenzy. The two large Mexicans were cleaning their Home Depot tools and smiling at him. Suddenly, one stepped up to him and shot three roofing nails from the nail gun into each of his shoulders. Rufkin choked on his screams.

"Tough-guy, your friend was brave but stupid. All we want to know is where is this guy they call The Lizard? He would only say he didn't know of his whereabouts. We know he was lying. Tell us and you will die quickly." They laughed and each took deep swallows of Tequila. Both bottles were nearly empty.

Rufkin used all his strength to try to rip the duct tape from his hands. His muscles reached a crazed level of power. He felt the tape stretch using the heels of his hands as leverage to gain some slack in the duct tape. The tape had not been applied professionally as the palms and thumbs had been left free to form a wedge which allowed extra pressure to stretch the material. A professional job would have secured the thumbs tight to the palm of the hand. Just as he felt the hope of freedom two nails hit both of his knee caps. He again choked on his scream.

The taller of the two ripped the tape off of Rufkin's mouth. Blood and spit flew in every direction. "Any answers for me tough little brown man? My next nails go into your balls and dick. You partner passed out when we did that to him."

Rufkin tried to speak, but choked on vomit. The two laughed and came at him with their nail guns. Rufkins strained and felt the tape again stretch. As the two came closer to finish their work, he kicked the smaller one in the balls, broke his neck with a quick flick of his wrists, and grabbed his nail gun. He instantly put four nails into the frontal lobe of the bigger Mexican.

The large man stood frozen as the control center of his brain sent flashes of excruciating pain through his body. He was twitching because of the multiple confused messages from the dying brain. He fell heavily against Rufkin. He put three nails directly into Rufkin's heart. Rufkin's face went blank. The two fell dead groping to each other.

SCOTT SAT SILENTLY IN THE HOT TUB LOCATED on the deck adjacent to his bedroom. He watched the sun set, smelled the late fall cool air and felt his skin tingle as the cooling air of dusk settled around him. The thin layers of strata clouds in the west were blazing orange.

"Jane, thanks for being here. This was a special evening. You were a lot of help. Planning the wedding for my backyard was a great idea. I didn't know Valli could be a romantic. The tents, the fire pits, the music, and the stars will be perfect for a wedding. By the way, thanks for the idea of this hot tub sunset skinny dip. Was this something you folks from Forest City did all the time?"

"How did you guess? All of the nude parties, skinny dipping and wife switching got to be so very old. That's why I had to leave." She giggled and slowly sipped her Wild Horse Chardonnay. Her deep brown eyes were frozen on his eyes. Her well endowed chest took a couple of quick deep breathes. His eyes involuntarily left her eyes and shifted to her breasts. They bounced in the bubbling water like two fishing bobbers on a windy day. There are some instinctive movements that even educated mature men cannot control. The toes of her left foot slowly wiggled up Scott's leg and stopped in his crotch.

"My God lady! What are we doing wasting time shriveling up in this hot water when there are more interesting things to do? Some parts of me have stopped shriveling and seem to be growing."

She nodded and gave him a wink and coy smile.

After a lustful excursion to his bedroom, they dressed and started the fireplace. "I have a new bottle of Panther Creek's red blend if you are interested. My old partner from Oregon sent it to me last week."

He put his hands around her shoulder as he delivered her wine, kissed her neck, and whispered in her ear. "Thanks for being here making me feel alive again. Isn't it great to feel like a teenager? Although, if I recall right, as a teenager I would never have known how to satisfy a cougar like you. I would have been only concerned with satisfying myself as quick as possible and as often as possible."

She paused, took a deep breath and nodded. She raised her glass. "May we enjoy many more tomorrows."

He sat and took a sip. "I have never seen Mindy so filled with anticipation. I hope the age difference between she and Valli never becomes a problem. I am always concerned. I wonder if she has ever thought what he would look like in a walker with oxygen tubes out of his nose while she is just in her early middle age?"

"Likely she hasn't had those thoughts. When you're young and in love no one thinks about those words , For Better or Worse. Certainly no one thinks what that word Worse can mean. When you are young, you always assume you will live together forever. You never think about living alone some day." Jane's eyes became misty.

"Let's stop. We both have known the crazy emotions of a caretaker and watching a spouse die before their time. Put it behind us? We can't change that. Let's talk about how much fun we had tonight. Snyder was the old Snyder. His new lady friend is a real hoot and a change of pace for him. She is nearly his age, smart, charming, and loaded. It's a big change for Snyder. He was usually into young, slow, sexy, horny, and broke.

Jane grinned. "Fielding's new boyfriend was interesting. He is quite the cook and bronze artist. He and Fielding seem like two little old friends who have known each other for years."

She continued, "What was Snyder meaning when he kept saying 'Old faithful is fully functional?' I assume he was referring to his over developed sexual prowess that he is always bragging about? You old men over-compensate."

"I know. You're right. We aging men are strange creatures. We are always afraid of diminished sexual drive, reduced sexual attraction and disappointing performance. We do talk big to cover up secret fears. In his case, he has been a basket case since his prostate surgery. I think Jackie has helped him regain his confidence."

The phone rang. "Valli, it was a great day, great plans, great drinks, great food, and be quick as I'm busy trying to get laid again."

Scott listened. His face lost its grin. He grew serious. "I will be at your place for coffee tomorrow at eight. Is everyone else set?"

THE AROMA OF THE FRESHLY PRESSED COFFEE filled Valli's kitchen. Mindy had long ago gone to work. No one was hungry. Everyone was jittery. They all knew there was a loose end still putting them at risk. Jesse was a witness and might figure them out.

"We have a break." Valli looked at all three of them.

"Snyder's computer program has been tracing flights from Cabo by Lear Jets like Garcia uses. One went to Minneapolis last week and has stayed there for three days. Those planes typically don't just hang around."

"Snyder's newspaper searching program has been looking for violent deaths in the Midwest states involving Eastern Europeans, Mexicans, or scruffy little white guys. In addition, he has imbedded a bug into the police system of every major town in the Midwest and there state's CBI. Wonder if that's a crime? Last night the system had a hit. The Minneapolis PD found a bunch of dead people from an apparent drug fight; two Bosnians, two woman and two Mexicans. It occurred in the art gallery area of Minnesota which was not a likely place for a drug shoot-out. I am guessing they are after Jesse. Remember the two dark Eastern European looking guys who were always hanging around him?"

Valli took a long sip of the strong black coffee. "This morning I called Walz who is testing drone jockeys at the Williston, North Dakota base. He took one of his drone training flights over the different airports in the Minneapolis area. At the St. Cloud airport he found it. The numbers on the Lear are the same as the one that came to Omaha for that Grand Opening party that we kind of helped ruin a few weeks ago."

Fielding scratched his perpetually disheveled curly hair. "What can we do to find out about these dead guys?"

Valli smiled. "I sent Jock on the road last night. He has a special female detective on the Minneapolis police force whom he called. It was a grizzly scene. Lots of torture and strange deaths. He snuck me a cell picture of the two dead Bosnians. I am convinced they were Jesse's body guards. Snyder agrees after reviewing the pictures we have of Jesse at his cave with those big guards.

Valli slowly sipped the deep black coffee. "Jock also found out that both of them had disposable cell phones. The police have deposited the phones in the evidence bin. Fielding, can you or Snyder figure out how we can tap those phones so we get any incoming calls before they just ring in the evidence bin?"

Fielding smoothed his hair. "It's funny you would ask that. Long ago, I worked on a device to attach to my boyfriend's cell phone so I could check on him. He was a cheating asshole. It's pretty simple. All you need is to insert a small router into the phone so it will send the signal elsewhere and not to that phone. I may have a few of them someplace. I could never figure out any practical use."

"Find those little routers and Scott and I are off to meet Jock in Minnesota. We need to get those routers installed. I need to call Mindy and tell her we are on a bachelor trip. Snyder do you have any way to trace a call even if it's from a throw away phone?"

"The disposable phones are over rated. If you are on them long enough, the coordinates can be fixed. The problem is most of the public police systems take a couple of minutes to triangulate. If you can't keep them talking you are SOL. I will hack into the state, county and city systems here and in Minneapolis to see what systems they have. Don't expect much."

Scott and Valli made the trip to Minneapolis in record time of three hours. Fielding's new police radar detection system told them if a police radar had been activated within a five mile range and pin-pointed the location. The location was then marked on the navigation system in Scott's car. Fielding again had a very marketable product.

Jock met them and took them to Hennepin Avenue and the main police station. He called his Detective friend and convinced her to let them review the items in the evidence bin. While Scott inserted the routers, Jock kept Detective Helga Ross occupied with questions about where they should all go for dinner.

That night Jock was obsessed with his planned seduction of Detective Helga. Her six foot frame put her at eye level with Jock. Her broad shoulders from Norwegian genes stressed the seams of her blue blazer. She obvious had worked hard at her weight issues as her legs were long and shapely. Her short well-coifed hair showed she cared for her looks, and the makeup was perfect in proportion. Jock was in a state of lust.

After dinner and too much wine, Jock found himself alone with her. It was 10 o'clock and Scott and Valli were long gone to bed. He slipped his hand on Detective Helga's thigh.

Jock leaned over and whispered, "Let's get reacquainted?"

She smiled. "I think my wife Ruth would frown on that. We are committed."

Jock smiled, nodded, and finished his drink in one move. Last time he was with her two years before, she was a lusting crazy animal. Could he have performed so bad she turned to Ruth?

Another aging male ego shattered.

CHAPTER TWENTY-EIGHT

" I Am Free Of Prejudices. I Hate Everbody Equally. "

W.C. FIELD

✶✶✶✶✶

JESSE AND STELLA HAD SPENT the last few days in the hotel. They had watched every currant movie release, played video games, and talked about their future. They were bored. Both were still puffy, but out of the bandage stage of their recovery.

He stood before the mirror. "I think when this swelling goes down, I will let my beard grow a little, and get one of those scruffy-look haircuts. I think I could look like that guy in Money Ball, Brad Whathisface. Do ya agree?"

"Oh, sure. You would be a dead ringer. I think I should get a few tattoos and earrings. I could be like Lisbon in the Dragon Tattoo movie, right?"

"I got to try Rufkin again. He hasn't answered his phone and that's not like him."

The call went unanswered.

She got on her new computer. She started going through the news for the Minneapolis area. After a few minutes of searching, she gasped. "I have our answer. We have to get the hell out of here now!"

The computer screen was filled with a story from the day before. It referred to a drug deal gone bad. Two Mexican men, two woman, and two Eastern European men were dead. The details and names were missing, but the details about a gory scene were mentioned. Stella rolled into a crying wailing ball of misery. Her brother and a dear friend were dead.

They quickly packed their bags and caught a cab to a used car lot. Jesse picked out a non-descript 2005 gray Dodge Dakota pickup. The only requests were good tires, a good motor and a good radio. The cash made the seller hurry along the paper work and temporary plates were issued to Rex Rice. They were both nervous and silent. They knew Garcia somehow had found them.

The trip up I-94 to Brainerd was full of emotions; tears, fears and anger resonated through the cab. A brief stop at the Brainerd Wal-Mart provided them with plenty of new clothes to help blend into the Gull Lake area. They also bought enough food and Miller's beer for a few weeks of privacy.

Jesse hit Highway 371 and headed to Nisswa. "I got a great place by Lake Roy. I bought it a few months ago for a safe house. Nisswa is a little town of about 1900 people. It has a lot of fishing, golf and tourist until October. After that it's a ghost town. I figured next spring I could learn to be a caddy and a fishing guide until we figure out our lives. Maybe I will take up golf! It looks easy. What do you want to do?"

"I think I will do nothing but eat and get fat. Maybe if you behave, I'll screw you on occasion."

For the first time they laughed.

The cabin was typical of a thousand others in Crow Wing County with is hundred plus lakes. Its uniqueness was its location. It sat on a point and could only be approached along a tree lined trail that opened to a rough rock walk 30 yards from the entrance. It was surrounded on three sides by water.

The other differences were the cameras in the trees watching approaching traffic, the alarms in the perimeter to detect approaching visitors, and the cabins interior. The log exterior structure was covered with moss and looked very in need of attention. The fireplace chimney was cracking and leaning. The shutters were unbalanced. The roof had batches of sites where the shingles had long ago blown away.

Inside it was filled with every electronic device that he wanted for his safety and pleasure. It also had a gun cabinet with five revolvers, two hunting rifles with large night scopes, and a semi-automatic AK47. The cellar, directly under the cabin, led to a boat house where a Lund 15 foot boat sat with a new 75 horse power Honda motor. An escape by water was easy.

The next few days they wandered the area. They tried pastries at the Chocolate Ox, biking on the Paul Bunyan Trail, breakfast at the Storehouse Coffee Shop and dined at the Grand View Lodge. Jesse was hooked on walleye filets. This business of hiding out was proving to be fun. They also became even better friends. They talked about the area, their future, and the sadness and anger for their loss. They often held hands in silence and looked at the sun set slowly over the lake and listened to the lonely cry of loons.

A week later, Jesse rushed into the cabin where Stella was working on a coconut encrusted walleye dinner. "I got Henry. He is in Brainerd. I told him to head to North Dakota and get a job in the oil fields. I reminded him to live simply and wait for my call. I don't get how they found Rufkin and Otto. We were so careful. Whatever I am missing, we can't afford to miss again?"

IN CABO, GARCIA was now dried out but in a nonstop rage. He had lost millions. He was embarrassed. The Lizard had gotten away. Carla kept him under her control, but kept his anger seething.

Without any feeling, she patted him on the forehead as he rested on his couch. "We were lucky to find the two body guards in Minneapolis. They still had the bags with the money. The tracking devices in the handles were still active but very weak. If they hadn't kept them in their room near a window we would have never found them. It unfortunate they told us nothing and your two cousins were killed. They were careless."

Garcia said, "Carla, what now? He is out there. I need to kill him. I still dream about him. I still see lizards walking out of the sea in my nightmares."

"Relax, Kurt. I have 50 men driving the roads of Minnesota to try and get a signal from Jesse's bags. If he is still using them, we will find him. They are talking to all the locals about new people who have moved to town. We will try Wisconsin next."

"Carla, I don't get your coldness. You haven't entertained me for weeks. What's up?

"You have been crazy, dirty, smelly and wacked out on meth. Does that give you any hints why there has been no sex? Get The Lizard and stay straight, and we will see what happens."

AFTER TWO WEEKS, a Garcia team reported a few blips from a fading tracking devise near various locations around Brainerd, Minnesota.

Carla entered the room in black filmy robe. She slid under the covers and reached for him. "Garcia, get your sorry ass up, get a few clothes on, and grab a couple of guns. You and your slow-witted over-muscled guys are going hunting in northern Minnesota for a reptile."

She gave his crotch a playful pat and tug. He smiled and reached for her. She slid to him. After he was satisfied, she laid out the plan for him.

Garcia was excited with the prospects of killing. After the surprise visit from Carla, he dressed and hurried out the door. He picked his three best muscle-men, headed to the airport and flew to Brainerd. His men in the northern Gull Lake area had just located a recurring faint beep from several locations in the Nisswa area. A quick trip to Nisswa and a few dollars to the locals produced a hand-drawn road map to the cabin that the locals said a new couple had just occupied. No one could recognize the pictures of Jesse or Stella. He was confused.

Garcia was never one to waste time with detailed plans. A head-on assault with semi-automatic guns was his only plan. If he killed the wrong people. he didn't care.

VALLI, FIELDING, SNYDER, and Scott were just finishing an early morning 50 mile bike ride to Ankeny and back to Woodward on the Old Trestle Trail. The new pavement made the ride easy. The trees were in full color transition as green turned to red and gold. As always, they paused half way across the bridge.

Scott took a deep breath of the fall air, filled with the aroma of harvest: cut crops, plowed fields, and diesel fumes from screaming harvest machines. "I look out cross the valley from up here and can imagine what was going through Tim's mind when he did the header off of here. He certainly picked a quick method. No turning back after the first step."

Fielding sniffed. "Can you image the fear he was going through knowing he was slipping, and yet at sometimes not even knowing where he was or why he was there? I cannot imagine the frustrations of going in and out of control or the embarrassment at realizing the things that you are doing are so bizarre. Remember at our last dinner how he was eating the salad with a spoon and dipping the bread in the wine?"

Silence descended on them. They all looked around and shook their heads.

Snyder's phone barked a cavalry charge sound.

"My system just signaled. Garcia's Lear has just filed a flight plan from Cabo to Brainerd with arrival late today. I think Jesse will be having guest for dinner. This fits with those quick calls to the two dead guys' cell phones in the MPD evidence bins. I have the router tied into the Minneapolis Police tracking system as if I were one of the agents. The five calls came from north of Brainerd, but they were so brief, I can't be specific."

Valli paused. "Scott, your biggest client has a Citation, so call him and let's see if we take a joy ride to Brainerd. We might beat them."

The trip from Des Moines to Brainerd was filled with silence. Scott and Valli applied dark colored hair spray and false mustaches to make them look much younger. Valli's plan was clear. He wanted to wait and watch the end to this story. He gave Scott two Glocks with silencers, a leather covered Sap, and a fold out knife.

Valli, asked, "Know how to use these?"

"Yes, I can use them. But I don't want to. This was to be a simple project, stop the merger. Not let's kill the leaders just for good measure. This is a little more than I bid for!"

"We aren't going to kill them. These weapons are for our safety. I just need to let them play it out, kill each other, and report the job completed. More importantly, I want us all safe from revenge. Garcia or The Lizard likely have figured out all of the explosions in the cave weren't just their doing. We all have a lot of years to live. I don't want to be looking over my shoulder."

The sleek white with black striped Citation taxied on the small tarmac of the Brainerd airport. A gangly pimple-faced long-haired flight attendant in jeans and red and black plaid wool shirt ran to help them.

"Park at the far end away from that Lear," Valli directed the Pilot.

The attendant took their bag and introduced himself as Elmer.

"Thanks for the help Elmer. When did that Lear arrive? Were there two guys in it?" Valli handed him a $20 dollar bill.

"Thanks for the tip. The Lear got here about half an hour ago. There were four very unfriendly Hispanics in it. They leased a car and got directions to Lake Roy. Poor tippers."

Valli and Scott looked like every day hip Minnesota executives in their designer jeans, turtle neck sweaters and brushed suede jackets. Valli wandered to the Lear and admiringly touched it while applying four tracers to its body.

As they approached the rental car kiosk, Scott was silent. Valli announced, "I am Vaughn James. I have a car rented for the day. Here's the credit card and driver's license."

Scott took a double take at the Vaughn James license and credit card.

The chubby young blonde lady hardly looked at the cards and slowly but precisely filled out the paperwork. Her tight jeans were stretched and her deep cut top showed ample cleavage. She winked at Valli. "You young men need any direction? How about suggestions for food or fun?"

"I think we are all set, Betty," Valli said as he looked at her name tag. "But where would you suggest we could get a drink later?"

"Join me and my girl friends at the Antlers in Nisswa. This time of year its double shots from 4 till 7:30 plus walleye nugget appetizers. The mayo dip is great."

As they got into the rusting blue 2002 Chevy Blazer, which was the last rental car, Scott laughed. "You are so full of shit. Where did you come up with the new name, license and credit card? Is that normal for retired USDA agricultural consultants? On second thought, don't answer that. I don't need or want to know!"

After a few miles Scott lost his sour look and started to laugh. "You just cannot help flirting with everything with a big rack and tight jeans. Will that ever stop when you're married?"

"You lawyers ask too many questions. As for the flirting, I just feel the need to keep in practice. It makes me feel young. Flirting is good for the soul and self image. You ought to try it. Maybe you can keep Jane interested longer than the others you have chased away?"

The trip to Lake Roy was quick. The old Jeep did not have a GPS, so a couple of brief stops were necessary for directions. Luckily, there were plenty of people out getting their places shut down for winter. Wood was being piled, windows were being covered with plastic, snow fences were being installed, and snow blowers were being tuned up. Each stop reported a SUV loaded with loud Hispanics a few minutes ahead of them.

They finally found the dirt road and slowly started to drive up it. A surprise was in store.

CHAPTER TWENTY-NINE

"Always Forgive Your Enemies. Nothing Annoys Them So Much."

OSCAR WILDE

*****

JESSE HAD JUST FINISHED filleting the three walleyes, when the alarm located at the northern entrance started to beep. Someone had just left the paved road and was starting down the rough dirt road to his cabin.

He ran at full speed to his office to view the monitor for that area. He played back the last few seconds. It displayed four dark complexioned men in an SUV rapidly headed his way.

"Honey, we have some unwelcomed company for dinner. Grab that big old duffle bag, a couple of rifles, and pistols. Go wait in the boat room! I will greet them."

She moved like a scared cat and did as directed. She felt a flash back of running from the death squads in Bosnia. Her breath became quick and shallow. She held one of the pistols very close, repeatedly flipping the safety as she hid in the shadows of the boat room.

Jesse actually was smiling and as he checked the cabin's living room and followed Stella down the steps to the boat room. He slowly dropped the boat from the hoist, unbuckled the lift straps and eased it down the rails into the water. Listening intently, he dialed his cell phone into the front door monitoring system which allowed him to see everything as if he was at the front door.

GARCIA WAS HYPER. He kept touching his pistol, grabbing his crotch and reopening his long switchblade. Sweat rolled down his temple. His dark eyes were dancing from the surge of an adrenalin rush and meth flashback. He could see the old dirty Dodge pickup setting in front of the cabin. The birds and insects were quiet. The air was heavy from an impending storm. Cumulus clouds built in the west. Lightening was dancing across the western sky followed by a deep rumble.

Garcia held up his hand. "Stop! Leave the car here in the trees. That opening would set us up like targets if he is waiting. We will slip along the side of the road using the trees as cover. When we run out of cover you three rush the door. Kill everyone in there. I am going around back in case there is another door."

The three Garcia cousins were now sweating. Their black shirts and sports coats became soaked when they heard their assignment to rush the front door while their boss checked the back door. They were cheese in the trap. They moved with silence that was unusual for six foot 250 pound men.

Running out of tree cover, the three rushed across the twenty yards open area in front of the cabins, brushed by the old pick-up, kicked open the door, and ran inside. It was empty. The TV was still on, the dish water still in the sink, and dirty dishes on the table. They let their weapons fall to their side and smiled. They picked up the note on the table.

"SURPRISE KURT!!!!"

Jesse watched their entrance and toggled the switch twice as his tongue swept rapidly across his lips. The three Claymore mines hidden in the open rafters of the cabin erupted. Fragments of steel shot downward in every direction. The three were instantly reduced to three mound of human salsa.

Garcia was rounding the corner to the back of the cabin just as they explosion ignited. An oar hit him hard in the stomach and then the head. He was groggy, but saw someone the size of Jesse shoot out of the boat house with the boat at full throttle. He had a woman with him. The face was confusing.

Garcia recovered, looked inside at what was once his three cousins, and staggered to his car. His rage sent him into black uncontrolled screams. He drove as hard as he could down the rough dirt road, leaving a swirling cloud of dust.

"Carla, we failed. Three more cousins are dead. I am headed to the plane. How do I get him? He must die"

"Relax Kurt, I have them on my tracking screen. They are crossing Lake Roy. They still have the bags with the tracers. We will get them. Come on home until we figure out our next move."

VALLI WAS QUIET ON THE RETURN FLIGHT. "Hard to tell who or how many were in that cabin when the claymores went off. Must have been quick. It clearly happened a few minutes before we arrived. The mounds were very fresh."

Scott was ashen color and shaken. "I am done with this. It has to be over. They must have gotten him. I am not cut out for this. I want that boring life with bad golf, good food, crazy wealthy clients, and lovely women."

"We are done Scott. I will collect our fee. Let's go get me married, and we will never get involved in this type of thing again. Okay?"

Scott toke a long drink from a mini bottle of vodka in the plane's bar. He took three more and passed one to Valli. "Think it will be long before the authorities find that mess?"

"It will likely be months. There is no reason for local people to go out there in the fall. The police are entering their relaxed season with no tourists to ticket for speeding or arrest on DUI. There is no reason for people to check on the occupants. Could be months before the smell tips someone off. Relax. It's over."

Valli knew he was lying, but needed to handle everything alone from now. He only had two weeks before his marriage. This assignment needed quick closure. He had a new life ahead of him. The honeymoon trip to Palermo and then to Taormina had Mindy thrilled. For Valli, it was nostalgic trip back to his roots. He likely would slip away and see a few relatives. Mindy could never know them.

He was changing. He knew it. The thrill of the hunt wasn't there. As they approached the cabin at Lake Roy, he had noticed the cameras in the trees and the laser alarm systems. He professionally avoided all of them leaving Scott behind to guard the road. More importantly, to get him out of the way if there was a problem. As he approached the cabin from the farthest possible direction along the north shore line, the endorphin rush wasn't there. He was feeling something new to him: fear.

He needed to keep his friends further away from this process. Valli never told them that when the switch for the rocket was activated the cave was full of innocent workers. He had merely shared the picture of Jesse rolling out of the cave and the sight of the explosion. He needed to wrap this up immediately and leave no witnesses behind.

CHAPTER THIRTY

"Age Is An Issue Of Mind Over Matter. If You Don't Have A Mind, It Doesn't Matter."

MARK TWAIN

*****

THE WEEK BEFORE THE WEDDING WAS FILLED WITH parties, good friends, well wishes, and ample second-guessing. Valli had never gone this far. He knew she made him feel young and alive. He felt like a teacher with a favorite student as he slowly spilled out his knowledge and experience gained over many years. She made him feel like a teenager when she flirted and tantalized him with the promise of sex. Besides being a tremendous flirt, she was also good on the follow through. She was beautiful, good natured, trusting and sweet. He knew he could never find her match. She gave him reasons to stay young, think young and grow old chromatically but not mentally. Knowing all of this, why was he scared?

Mindy had decided that this week they would abstain from sex. She, in fact, moved into a single friend's home. Valli could not understand the female thought process. They had been passionate lovers for nearly a year. They were aggressive lovers. How was this one week going to make things better? Valli just left the subject alone. Why have a debate over a subject he would never understand? Female logic on this subject was clearly a contradiction of terms.

He rather enjoyed the evenings of solitude of have a glass of good White Oak Reserve Blend, looking over the meadow below his condo at Owl's Head, and feeling the pure fall air descend on him. He knew he had to bring an end to his past life. He could not put her at risk. He could not put his friends at risk.

On his third night alone, his computer gave an unusual horn sound. The horn signaled that the system Snyder had developed was reporting the filing of a flight plan by a Lear from Cabo. He quickly activated Snyder's program that showed all such flight plans from Cabo. He was startled. The destination was Des Moines with arrival tomorrow at ten. He checked the tracing devises he had fixed to the Lear's hull. It was motionless, and was located some place on the small private airstrip north of Cabo San Lucas.

Valli dialed his cell. "Walz, sorry it's late. This deal may be coming to an end. Can you have a drone up from North Dakota and in the Des Moines area on one of your practice flights tomorrow morning? By the way, can you load one of those hummingbird drones on it for some close up work? Can you arm those old drones?"

"I have one hummingbird left that I haven't wrecked yet. Harriet IV is my last one. Those young guys are a lot better with a joystick than me. No, I cannot arm the drone. After five wrecks, they hardly trust me with extra fuel."

"Just be there. It's best you stay uninformed. Keep your cell by your side."

VALLI SAT PATENTLY IN THE OBSERVATION parking area at the end of McKinley on the northeast side of the Des Moines airport. He watched as planes came in for landing on runway number 31 which was being used that morning. Finally Garcia's Lear arrived a few minutes after ten and taxied to the Elliott Terminal. Valli slipped on his coveralls and Iowa Cubs' hat.

As Garcia and the three Mexicans came through the terminal gates, Valli casually browsed around the paperwork on the desk and found which car they had rented. He drove it to the exit door acting as a good valet. It was full of gas and was equipped with two new tracing devises.

"Hey, little old man. Get a map and show me where Boone is."

Valli responded and showed the long route through Ames to Boone. The Denali SUV shot out of the entrance, turned left on Fleur Drive and sped to I-235. Valli headed west to take a shortcut on R22 and R29 to Boone.

Valli called on his cell. "Walz, head for Boone. How long before your there?"

"Ten minutes, and Boone is in my drone's sights."

THE CABIN NEAR BOONE was located near the small town of Moingona adjacent to the Ledges State Park in the rolling wooded hills of central Iowa. Jesse had spent several times at this safe house. He loved to wander the hills quietly watching the game. It was much like his Loess Hills. He felt at home and safe.

It was a modest one-story log cabin on the outside: rough cut logs, shake shingles in growing disrepair, a porch with a swing on the front, no grass, just weeds, and a tilting rusting metal chimney. Inside it had Jesse's taste for great electronics and guns. It sat on the top of a hill with a half mile narrow timber lined road leading to its front. Jesse had added his usual warning systems plus cameras located in the trees.

In addition, in the front approach to the house Jesse had dug two hidden bunkers that were connected by bush-lined pathways. They each had cleared areas for killing zones. The back of the house could only be accessed by climbing up a 300 foot shale outcropping.

Stella made several trips to the Boone Wal-Mart and quickly added her touch. She felt as if they had found a permanent home. He knew she was premature. Garcia would be back. He had placed all the empty Pioneer Seed duffle bags in a pile in the tool shed attached to the north side of the cabin. They were perfectly in his killing zones.

She asked over coffee one morning, "Will he find us?"

"No doubt he will. Those Pioneer bags gave me the answer as to how Otto and Rufkin got caught. They came from Garcia and were always close to all of us. Each one has a little button inserted in them which I believe is a tracing devise. I busted one open and it is filled with wires and a small battery."

He gave her a big reassuring hug. "We just wait and end it here."

She quietly assembled her get away bag and a duffle bag of money. She was a survivor. She had done whatever was necessary several times before. She desperately hoped she would not escape alone. The little hillbilly had grown on her. Despite his early rough and tumble years, he was now sweet, thoughtful, and cared for her. He was even smart enough to know on a holiday when she said she wanted nothing that she was not being truthful. He knew she was really saying "Surprise Me, but get me something." Not every man has figured out that message.

Every morning Jesse went for quiet walks, repeatedly checked the cameras and cleaned his favorite rifle. He knew the time was close. Each night they sat and talked about the sky, the sunset, their plans, and the future. He was strangely at peace and desperately wanted to live.

CHAPTER THIRTY-ONE

"A Man Cannot Be Too Careful In His Choice Of Enemies"

O SCAR W ILDE

✶✶✶✶✶

THE NIGHT WAS QUIET AND SERENE. Turkey and quail were quietly milling about feeding on the acorns and seeds that had recently dropped. Several deer watched as Stella and Jesse sat on the porch sipping beer and munching chips. The deer just grazed and watched. They felt safe.

"How will this all play out?"

"I figure they park their car at the bottom of the road and slip up here through the timber. I doubt they use the road after their last experience. They will be tracking the signal from those bags in the shed. They won't use the cliff behind us as an approach. It's too steep. I will have plenty of warning from the alarms and cameras. First I will go to that bunker to my right and take out the farthest two. My .243 caliber Winchester has a silencer and the bullet delivery is quick. The next two will hardly know what is happening."

Jesse was fidgeting with excitement. "After hitting the first ones, I then set off the wounded turkey call in the first bunker and run like hell through the tree-line till I am in the next bunker to their left. As they sneak to the sounds of the call, I just go pop and pop. This old gun doesn't miss."

"I hope you are as good as that plan sounds. When this is all over, what's next?"

"I have been thinking about using this new name and clean record of Rex Rice and going to school here in Boone. The area college has a degree in law enforcement that interests me. Can you see me as Sherriff Rex? Some small town will love a handsome stud with my sense of justice and fair play."

She tried to hold in the laugh, but failed. "Do you think you could stay on the right side of the law for long?"

"I'm serious. I understand a lot more than I used to. Pot is one thing. In small use it isn't much different than whiskey, but most people can't keep it small. Meth is another thing. There is no such thing as a little. I watched my whole sales force become a bunch of jittery, sniffing idiots in a few months. I could do some good keeping it out of a town. I don't know if I can keep it out and also follow the law though. Old habits are hard to break."

"What does Mrs. Rex Rice want with her new life?"

"I think I am off to college. I want to know all I can about computers and their future. Drake University is in Des Moines and has a big reputation. Iowa State in Ames is twenty miles away and has great academics. My other option is to hide in these hills and be the paid whore for a good looking multimillionaire like you."

The two held hands and watched the full fall moon rise and light up the night. They had found their soulmate. Their puffy faces and sore necks from the surgery had healed. Jesse was looking forward to a good night.

JESSE WAS UP EARLY. Hearing the beeping signal, he checked the security systems, the camouflage on the bunkers and his favorite rifle. His apprehension was appropriate. The SUV stopped at the base of the hill and the four men dressed in green and tan desert gear removed their weapons; small snub-nosed Polish automatic machine guns that would dispense 20 shots a second and carried 100 round magazines.

They spread out with two on each side of the trail and commenced to climb through the trees to the log cabin on top of the hill.

He watched with amusement. He crept to his first bunker.

Felix Mantia and Juan Pablo were on the right. They hugged the ground while moving forward rapidly in a crouched walk. Their eyes flitted about the trees and bushes above them which were transparent as the fall had caused them to drop their leaves. They quietly moved through the layers of red and yellow leaves, trying to control the sound of their deep breathing.

Felix and Juan were cousins of Kurt Garcia. They had grown up together in Acapulco. In their early years they loved the beauty of the beaches on the Bay of Lucia. As they grew older Hans Garcia summoned them to make the 200 mile trip to Mexico City. They were trained in self defense and killing methods. Their ridged training program was paramilitary in nature. By the age of eighteen they were accomplished thugs who enforced the Garcia enterprises business in Acapulco.

Felix smelled the grass, the clean air, and fear. He longed to be back swaggering down the beaches flexing his impressive muscle while shaking down the beach vendors who reported to him. He loved that life. Being a Garcia bad guy was his life.

Felix heard a thud. He turned and saw Juan lying motionless with the back of his head turning red. As he looked up, he felt a flash to his forehead. All his senses went black as the bullet blew his brains through the back of his skull.

Garcia and his long time guard Carlos took the left side of road. Using the same approaching techniques they were nearing the house. Garcia held the tracking devices. He was sweating more with anger and desire to kill than exertion. They stopped and froze when they heard the scream of a wounded or frightened turkey to their right.

WALZ PUT THE DRONE IN A FIXED CIRCLING PATTERN. The ground fog obstructed his vision from 5000 feet so he had released Harriet IV for a closer look at the events below.

"Valli, I can see five hot spots on the heat detection slope. Four are moving up the hill, one is quiet on the right side. Which one are you?"

"I am not on the chart yet, climbing up this shale cliff is a little harder than I thought. Hope Mindy will understand a few skinned knees and arms. I just topped the ridge, am I on your scope?"

"I see you on the ridge. Don't move, I think this is solving itself. The two on the right have stopped moving and the guy up the hill is running like hell to the left of the two guys on the left. I think our hillbilly is in ambush mode. Harriet has just gotten down there so I can get a visual. Shit, she hit a tree."

Valli ignored the direction to stay put and moved slowly down the hill moving using every tree and bush for cover. The thrill of the stalk was coming back. A rush of endorphins from the hunt was releasing. He had felt it many times, and each time it took him to height of awareness that made every nerve tingle and every sense operate at mach level.

"Valli, the two on the right are not moving and I can see through Harriet's camera what looks like blood on both heads. I am working Harriet through the trees to the guy on the left. Shit, I hit another tree head on. I hope this old bird is tough."

Looking through the side window of the cabin Valli saw a small dark-haired woman holding a Glock in both hands with a large duffle bag and two rifles standing beside her. He had to decide her fate later after he completed the project at hand.

"Shit! The two on the left are down and not moving. I am circling around looking for the sniper that pulled this off. I think I see him headed toward the cabin, but the compass in Harriet is malfunctioning and I am having control issues. That third tree I hit may have done some serious damage. Shit, make that the fourth tree. Get out of there! I am losing control. Her vision is now going on the blink."

JESSE SAT IN EXHAUSTION ON THE STEP. Sweat gushed from his pores in the cool of the fall morning. He leaned back, smelled the air, watched the fog parting overhead, and smiled. He at last felt inner peace. He was free, rich and in love. Stella rushed from the house and threw her arms around him. They embraced for well over a minute. A gasping "I Love You" escaped from Jesse.

They walked hand in hand to the porch where he collapsed in a slump. "I love you and want to get out of here and start a new life. I am never going to go through this stress again."

She hugged him and gave him a big kiss on the forehead. "Relax, Mr. Rice. I will get you a couple of cold beers before we do our cleanup work."

Standing in the shadow of the house within earshot of the couple, Valli looked at the shooter. He didn't look like the pictures that he had of Jesse. The nervous licking of his lips was a giveaway.

Valli's mind was racing. With a quick move, the injection of tetrodotoxin in his hand could be administered like it had been done dozens of times before. Jesse would instantly feel the venom of the Puffer Fish flashing through his nervous system. Organs would stop; first the diaphragm, then the lungs and then the heart. Death would be quick and irreversible. The poison would never be detected as it was not part of a normal toxicology screen and quickly dissipated.

Starting to glide forward to end his work. He stopped. He had never left a victim alive. But he had never been in love himself. He realized bad people can change and can love. He emptied the needle on the ground, quietly slipped around the cabin, and rappelled down the shale cliff. Jesse had been given a second chance, but he would never know it.

Stella and Jesse sat in silence. They held hands, shook their heads in disbelief and remained silent. Birds were just renewing their morning calls and feeding. The air was stirring as a fall rain storm began to move in from the west.

"We need to get rid of them and get the hell away from here. The people back in Mexico know where we are and more of them might come. We just eliminated their boss, so I expect more revenge. Can you get us packed and unplug the electronics. I need to run to town."

A quick visit to the Wal-Mart store provided 50 bags of cement, 50 bags of potting soil and several boxes of fall rye grass seed. He put two bodies into each of the bunkers he had created for his ambush. The bags of cement were sprinkled on them without water to assure quick decomposition. Soil was added as another layer. The fast growing seed covered by the falling leaves was the last touch. Animals would not bother the graves because of the concrete smell, and by spring they would be part of the landscape.

The couple loaded the old pickup with the electronics that had been removed from the cabin. The surveillance equipment was removed and boxed for use on another day. They headed to Boone where the electricity and water for the cabin was prepaid for a year.

The rental car lease showed the leasing company was Elliott Flying Service in Des Moines, so they headed south and during the night left it at their office. Jesse noticed the familiar Lear setting on the tarmac. He snuck under the fence and placed three bugs on the fold- up flaps covering the wheel wells during flight. He would keep track of the location of the plane for a long time.

Jesse and Stella hopped into his pickup and took I-29 south for three hours and left three Pioneer bags in the backroom of a gas station in North Kansas City. He then drove west to Wichita and left three more bags in the cleaning closet of a Holiday Inn Express off of exit 50. He continued west to Topeka and left three more in the furnace room of a Residence Inn.

The two were exhausted. They retraced their route back north and stopped at the first motel they could find. A steak dinner at Montana Mike's in Emporia Kansas was like a tranquilizer to them. They fell asleep entwined into each other. Jesse could not stop smiling with his new found-freedom. Now what??

CHAPTER THIRTY-TWO

CAROL LEIFER

✱✱✱✱✱

THE SMALL TRIO OF VIOLINS HAD JUST FINISHED. Their mellow notes hung in the air. The sun was just starting its descent in the west. The acres of prairie grass and flowers stood unwavering in the still-cooling air.

The small crowd of people stood as the violins struck the first notes of the bridal entrance theme. Mindy emerged from first level of Scott's home with her father, Richard, in tow. Her thin body was perfectly displayed in a strapless straight white dress which tastefully hugged every curve. The sequences on the bodice sparkled in the fading sunlight. Black long hair clung to her face and accentuated her large dark eyes.

Valli's wedding gift of four strands of pearls around her neck, sparkled in the fading sunlight. Her smile and glow were captivating.

After a few well-thought-out comments by a popular retired judge, the legally required commitments were concluded. Valli turned to the guest.

"It is rare that a man finds someone who in every way makes him happy. A warm smile over coffee, a brief touch as you dress, a hand squeeze as you part, a gaze of love over an evening wine and a simple kiss as you go to sleep. It seems so natural. Yet many people never have these sensations or appreciate them. It took me a lot of years to find what many people call love. Some people never find it. Please toast Mrs. Valli, my companion for life."

The wine flowed freely, the music softly danced across the prairie, and everyone was enjoying the seafood spread that Valli had flown in that morning. The Maine lobster, Russian caviar, and Alaskan crab were perfectly matched with the Dom Perignon Champaign.

Fielding gave Valli a big hug. "I hope sometime I will have the feelings you obviously have. I realize as you grow older having a partner to share the little but important moments of life with is crucial. By the way, while I look for that person, you made me a fortune. The idea of listening rocks and spy birds hit the fancy of the military. With their reduced budget, they are looking for anyway to eliminate people. I am going in to DC next week. Scott and I are negotiating a development contract with a nice upfront fee and royalties if they work."

As he turned Fielding winked. "By the way, count me out of your next consulting deal. I like my freedom. A jail cell with a horny disgusting guy not of my choosing is not on my bucket lists."

Walz's towering frame moved with his normal limp and engulfed Valli in a bear hug. He slipped a small bundle into Valli's hand. Valli started to laugh as he looked at the damaged hummingbird drone. Its beak was bent, one eye hung out, both wings were at odd angles and the head extended too far from the body.

Walz laughed. "Harriet IV died trying to get back from the shootout. By the way, you do move well for an old guy. I am done with this type of clandestine operations. I am also grounded from drone operations for destroying my limit of equipment."

" I hear you are moving back to Des Moines? All done with government consulting?

"I am a victim of the cutbacks. I have seen it before. The military will do with less people until the next crisis and a new President causes the patriotic light to again go one. Until then, I am working on a self-hypnotic program to allow a perfect takeaway of a driver, a deft touch with a wedge and a non-yippy putting stroke. I can make a fortune selling it to golfers who think they can buy a game. I am already feelings its effect."

They both laughed.

Walz gave another hug. "I envy you. Having a loving horny young lady by your aging decaying side as you grow old is my secret dream. I think our buddy Scott may have also found the real thing."

Both men looked as Scott walked hand in hand with Jane introducing her to his friends. They were both excited about a cruise to Greece and Italy scheduled for the following week.

I hope Jane's cruise has a better ending than the last one, Valli thought to himself.

As he stood alone looking into the last quarter of the sun slide below the thing clouds, Valli felt something new. He was at peace. He would find a new direction for his retirement planning.

CARLA WATCHED THE SUNSET behind the hills at The Pedregal. The view from the villa overlooking the Pacific Ocean was again perfect. A few distant sails bobbed on the calm sea. People walked the beach mesmerized by the huge evening swells crashing over the rocks below. She slowly put aside the huge book of financials and turned to Vaughn Mueller, the last board of director member of Garcia Enterprises.

"We lost over 20 million from that little effort. I think, however, we learned a lot. We need to try it again, but do it on our own. Mergers never seems to be easy. Strange little characters like Marvin are unpredictable. We also need to not work through a slow-witted mean spirited leader like Kurt. They are too hard to manage. I wonder where he went too? Likely he was a victim of The Lizard."

Carla turned to Mueller. Her eyes flashed with a fire.

"I know The Lizard is out there. He outsmarted Garcia, but I won't rest till we get him. We also need to figure out who else was involved in that third explosion and eliminate them. "

She gently moved her bare foot up the calf of the older man and gave him an impish smile. His stoic blue Teutonic eyes never blinked. A lecherous smile started to develop on Mueller's wrinkled face.

"You will make a wonderful President of Garcia Enterprises. I look forward many years of coaching you in our culture and future plans. Maybe a lovely young thing like you can teach me a few new things?"

Carla smiled and stroked his left hand. "I am likely to always be the student, but I will try to surprise you on a few occasions. I think this is one of those times."

She easily lured him to the bedroom; moving like a lioness leading her prey to her lair. Mueller jumped up, ignored the popping of his aging knees and followed. Like most men, he never once considered the price he would pay for this apparently free lay. Free sex often carries a big price tag.

THE HOME CLOSING WAS QUICK. Cash closings can move along red tape with ease. Jesse and Stella had used their second set of false identification papers. They were now Larry and Lorna Evens who had recently moved to Des Moines from Dallas.

She slowly walked around her new condo at Owl's Head. He walked into the park below their deck as the flakes of an early snow started to fall. It was perfect. South of Grand in a wooded area near the Water Works Park and 15 minutes from Drake University. They were a few minutes from the symphony's venue, the Civic Center and the Art Center.

He had explored his options and enrolled in the area college. His new identification showed he had a high school education and years of experience in the agricultural business. He had a clear interest in law enforcement and several local programs were available. He knew he could bring some real life education to the police force that hired him.

He felt the snow melting on his skin. He smiled and his eyes danced when he thought of how good he would be as an undercover agent. He also felt this career was a perfect place to keep an eye out for any intrusions from Mexico. They would never look for The Lizard on a police force.

Stella enrolled at Drake and to pursue a degree in computer business and internet communications. She felt this knowledge could lead to a new career of assisting new immigrants to this country in learning the language, adopting the culture and moving into the work force. She also thought of developing a system to warn them of any private planes leaving Mexico for this area. She still dreaded the possible reprisal of the Garcias.

She opened the bottle of Silver Oak Merlot, compliments of the realtor, smelled it and poured six ounces into a crystal glass. She walked out to the deck, leaned on the rail, took a big breath of winter air and a sip of the wine. The flowers and bushes below her were now brown and drab. The grasses were fading to a pale yellow. The tree's leaves were lying in multi colored heaps. She took another big sip and smiled as she watched her husband walk slowly in the falling snow. A smile was frozen on his face. He kept looking as the snow accumulated and kicking the piles of leaves like a little boy on a stroll.

She also was experiencing a serene feeling of being at ease, in love and rich. She knew it was a precarious situation. The hidden cameras need to be quietly planted. The surveillance warning system needed installation. The guns needed to be hidden, but handy, just in case the Mexicans did return.

She started to plan their lives. This was a luxury she had never enjoyed. They needed to act like middle-aged students, not display their money and make only a few acquaintances who did not ask too many questions. She looked forward to meeting their neighbors, especially the Vallis, the newlyweds the realtor had mentioned. The realtor mentioned the bride was expecting.

Stella knew they needed to silently slip into their new town's culture, enjoy a new life and never attract attention. This was a good place to hide. She sipped the last of her wine. Jesse turned, waved and yelled, "I am in love!"

Made in the USA
Charleston, SC
26 January 2013